ROLL BOUNCE LOVE

KAY SHANEE

B. LOVE PUBLICATIONS

ABOUT THE AUTHOR

Kay is a forty-something wife and mother, born and raised in the Midwest. During the day, she is a high school teacher and track coach. In her free time, she enjoys spending time with her family and friends. Her favorite pastime is reading and writing romance novels about the DOPENESS of BLACK LOVE.

SYNOPSIS

Dance instructor, Aubrielle Carson had her heart broken more times than she could count. Until she met the one. He was all she dreamed of at first, but with time and attention, she found he was just as disastrous as the loves before him. Ending the relationship left her with a need for change and relocating to Washington D.C. was the new beginning she craved. However, her hungry heart refused to remain unfed.

Rashaad Hanes was finally living the life he earned. As a single father and co-owner of Roll Bounce Love, a new skating rink in town, he was confident, focused, and about his business. All of that was what he intended to bring to the table when he approached the woman he couldn't take his eyes off of. Yet, despite all he came with, her guard was up.

Will Aubrielle give love another try? Is Rashaad forgetting to calculate his own flaws? When secrets and half-truths shake the ground, will these two lovers be able to roll with the punches and bounce back to love?

PROLOGUE

Aubrielle's Prologue

"I should have left the first time I caught his ass," I said to myself as I threw clothes into a suitcase.

When Damon and I started dating, he was the perfect boyfriend and felt like a dream come true. He was tall, dark, handsome, well built, college educated, and treated me like a queen. At the time, he was thirty-three and working his way up the corporate ladder at a finance company. He was different from the men I typically dated, which I thought was a definite plus. I tended to be attracted to thugged-out niggas, and Damon was the complete opposite; there was nothing thug about him. I truly thought I'd hit the jackpot. Being thirty-one, I was ready to settle down, possibly get married, and start a family.

About eight months into our relationship, I lost my job. I worked as a dance instructor at one of the hottest studios in Atlanta. I taught various dance types, but most of my clientele were strippers who worked at some of the most-popular strip clubs in the A. My pole dance classes were so popular that there was always a waiting list.

The owner was doing some fraudulent shit that caused the studio to be shut down, leaving me unemployed. Even though I had enough money saved to carry me for at least five to seven months, depending on how frivolous I was, I didn't hesitate to accept his offer when he invited me to move in with him. What I should have done was moved back in with my parents. They offered, but Damon and I were still in the honeymoon stage of our relationship, and I thought he was my knight in shining armor, so I moved in with him.

A month later, I ended up accepting a position at another dance studio. Because I was new, I had to teach the classes that nobody else wanted, but it was cool. The pay was decent, and I still was able to do what I enjoyed. Damon refused to let me pay any bills, which was another bonus of living with him, and my savings account continued to grow.

As soon as we hit the one year mark, everything went south. Women were sending me messages on Facebook, Instagram, and Twitter about their escapades. Some would send pictures, and others would send screenshots of text messages or DMs. It just goes to show you that all men have the potential to cheat, no matter the age, education, or upbringing.

Damon was a real smooth talker, though. Somehow, he managed to talk his way out of every single situation. Deep down, I knew his ass was up to no good. I'd gotten too comfortable with him taking care of me, and the thought of leaving seemed overwhelming. I lost track of how many times Damon cheated on me over the past two years, but it stopped today!

After packing four suitcases and three duffel bags, I requested an Uber to take me to the airport. My flight wasn't for five hours, but I wanted to be out of the house before Damon got home. Some days, he came home for lunch at noon, which didn't give me much time. It took a few trips, but I got all of my luggage to the end of the driveway. Turning on the alarm, I exited through the garage, leaving the house keys on top of the deep freezer.

Looking at the Uber app, I saw that it was still seven minutes away. While I waited, I FaceTimed my cousin Keyla, who I would be staying with until I found a place. She lived in Washington D.C.

"Hey! You at the airport?" she answered the call.

"No, not yet. I'm waiting for the Uber."

"Girl, I'm so excited. I can't wait until you get here. It'll be just like back in the day."

Keyla and I spent most of our teenage years together. When her parents were killed in a car accident, my parents gained custody of her. We were both fourteen at the time, and neither of us had siblings. When we graduated from high school, she decided to go to Howard University and loved D.C. so much that she never moved back to Atlanta. I decided to stay close to home and attended Emory University, majoring in dance.

"I know! But I promise I won't wear out my welcome at your place. I already have a few interviews lined up, and as soon as I get a job, I'll be out of your way."

"Cousin, please! I'm glad to have some damn company, and you can stay with me as long as you want."

"Oh shit! Key, let me call you back. Damon just pulled up."

"What? You make sure you call me right back. If you don't, I'm calling the police."

I ended the call and tucked my phone into my purse. Damon couldn't pull into the driveway because I had my luggage blocking it. He hopped out of his Benz with fire in his eyes.

"What's all this?" he asked, waving his hand in the air for emphasis.

Releasing a deep breath and rolling my eyes, I replied, "What does it look like?"

"It looks like you trying to leave me."

"My, my, my… aren't you perceptive?" I said, laced with sarcasm.

"I had a feeling you were up to something when you didn't get mad about those pictures. I swear—"

"Damon, don't even tune your mouth up to tell me another lie. I'm done! Now you can go fuck as many women as you want, and you don't have to worry about hiding it from me."

"Come on, Bri! I promise you. You don't have to worry about—"

"Aht, aht!" I held my hand up and shook my head. "We're done. I've given you way too many chances, and I'm tired. I thought you were my forever, but it's obvious I ain't who you want."

"You are, baby! I swear you are. Give me one more chance, and I promise you'll see a whole new man."

Thankfully, the Uber pulled up right behind his car. Ignoring his pleas, I picked up the two duffel bags that were on the ground and approached the vehicle. The driver popped the trunk, and I carefully placed those bags, along with the one I had on my shoulder, in the truck.

"Bri, you can't be serious right now. After all I've done for you, you're leaving me?"

Damon stood in front of the four suitcases and blocked me from getting them.

"Will you stop playing and get the hell outta my way?"

"No! Baby, let's just go inside and talk this out. I know you don't want to throw away the two years we've spent together over a misunderstanding."

"Misunderstanding?" I said with a frown. "There is no misunderstanding. I understand that you have a community dick. Your dick is for every-fucking-body. It's real clear to me. Now move, or I'm calling the police!"

He was slow to move at first, but when I took out my phone, he got his ass out of my way. I grabbed two of the suitcases and put them in the trunk. When I went back for the other two, he reached for me, and I slapped his hand away.

"Damon, the way these police officers out here shooting niggas at will, I would hate to have to call 911."

He released a deep breath and stepped away from me. After putting the last of my luggage in the trunk, I hopped in the back seat and threw up the deuces. *I'm already over that nigga!*

PROLOGUE

Rashaad's Prologue

"What kind of woman wakes up and decides she no longer wants to be a mother?"

"I never wanted to be a mother, and you know that, but you begged me to keep her. I've tried to embrace it, but I'm miserable, and I can't pretend anymore."

"Are you serious right now? This has to be a joke. Where the fuck is Ashton Kutcher?"

"It's not a joke, Rashaad! I can't do this anymore."

"I understand you not wanting to do *this* anymore. We've been living like roommates for years, and it's getting old, but you don't even give a fuck about leaving your daughter?"

"Honestly, if we didn't have Zara, our relationship would probably be much stronger. I've resented you since the day you convinced me to have her. Motherhood ain't for me, and I can't do it anymore."

"You're a piece of work, Carmen. I swear to God, I will never again in my life let my dick lead the way. Say what the fuck it is you trying to say. I need you to spell this shit out for me."

My patience was wearing thin, and Carmen was beating around the bush. I already knew what was up, but I needed to hear her say it, so there would be no misunderstanding on my part.

"I'm leaving, Shaad. If I stay, I'm gonna lose it, and that won't be good for any of us. I want to sign over all my rights to you."

"You don't even wanna co-parent? What kinda shit is that?"

"The kinda shit I've been wanting to do for the past six years. I've been pretending to be someone I'm not, sacrificing my happiness trying to do what everyone thinks is right, and I'm tired of it."

I shook my head in disbelief because as much as I couldn't believe what I was hearing, I could. As I tried to process the bullshit spewing out of Carmen's mouth, the past seven years flashed through my mind.

From the day we met, there was something about Carmen that my spirit didn't connect with, but, like a dumbass, I ignored it. She was beautiful, smart, independent, her pussy was top-notch, and she was a certified freak.

I let all of that cloud my judgment, continued to ignore my gut feeling, and before I knew it, we were in a full-blown relationship. Deep down, I knew we wouldn't stand the test of time, so when she told me that she didn't see marriage or children in her future, I didn't think much of it. At the time, I wasn't ready for any of that, anyway.

About three months into our relationship, she found out she was pregnant, and I had to beg her not to have an abortion. Although I knew Carmen wasn't my forever in my heart of hearts, I was willing to give it a shot for my seed. I felt her resentment of me, and my efforts to make it work failed. By the time Zara was about a year old, Carmen and I had separate bedrooms.

"What am I supposed to tell Zara?"

"I don't know. I know this might be hard for her, but she's a strong little girl. She'll—"

"She's five, and the only thing she'll think is that her mother doesn't love her."

"I do love her, but I love me, too. I've been neglecting my wants and needs since I found out I was pregnant, and I can't do that shit anymore. I got a new agent, and—"

"That's what the fuck this is about? Your new agent promised he could make you a star?"

"What he said doesn't matter. I can't be what Zara needs me to be. I don't have it in me. We aren't all that close, anyway. She probably won't even care that I'm gone."

"You're her mother, Carmen. Of course, she'll care. If this was your plan all along, I wish you would have left when she was a baby. She's gonna be devastated."

"I've been contemplating leaving for years. Mentally and emotionally, I've been gone for a long time. Zara was never supposed to happen. We talked about this before we got serious, and you were cool with it."

"I was cool with us not having children, but I was never cool with you aborting my seed once she was conceived. There's a difference."

"You're an amazing father, Shaad. You love her enough for both of us."

Shaking my head, I said, "You really need to be sure about this, because if you leave, you're making the biggest mistake of your life, and I promise you, ain't no coming back."

1

AUBRIELLE CARSON

Six Months Later

"Bri, will you hurry up? The line is gonna be around the corner by the time we get there if we don't leave soon."

My cousin Keyla had to be the most impatient person in the world. I was getting dressed as fast as I could. My last dance class of the day ran late, which caused me to get home late.

"Key, I'm moving as fast as I can. I'm trying to look cute so I can find me a new nigga," I yelled from my bedroom.

That wasn't exactly true. Although I wasn't looking for a man, I wouldn't mind going on a few dates. I'd been in Washington D.C. for six months, and I loved it. I could see why Keyla decided to make it her home. She and I thoroughly enjoyed being together again, and she constantly told me that I didn't have to rush to find a place. However, I'd been looking and hoped to find something soon. With the money I had saved and my current income, I wasn't too worried.

Groove Motion Dance School hired me on the spot a few days after I arrived in D.C., and it was my first time teaching all styles of dance to students who were under eighteen. I only taught adults in Atlanta and never thought I'd enjoy working with children, but I loved it.

"Shit, you and me both. That really shouldn't be a problem tonight. Everybody in town been waiting for this skating rink to open. Which is another reason why you need to hurry it up."

"Okay, okay! I'm ready."

I decided to wear a pair of dark denim, distressed jeans with a fitted, white graphic tank top bearing a picture of my favorite rapper, Tupac. It was still fairly warm out during the day for mid-September, but the evenings were a little cool. Hopefully, I wouldn't get too chilly in just the tank top.

"Damn, cuz! You got enough holes in them jeans? You showin' all that thigh meat tonight," she teased.

I looked down at my jeans and had to agree with her. Shrugging my shoulders, I said, "Lil' thigh meat ain't never hurt a soul. How you talking about me when you showing more than me?"

Keyla was wearing a pair of light-colored denim shorts, and they were short. With all that ass she was carrying behind her, she was sure to draw some attention. She paired it with a teal-colored T-shirt that stopped right underneath her breasts.

"True!" she said, followed by a laugh. "Damn, I almost forgot my skates. I'll be right back."

I adjusted my skates, which were draped over my shoulders while I waited for Keyla to get hers. "I haven't skated any since I moved here. I hope I'm not too rusty."

"I haven't skated in a while either, not since the rink I used to go to closed about a year ago."

"I guess we're about to find out. Let's go."

About forty minutes later, we were approaching the moderately long line.

"See, I told you there'd be a line."

"Well, we couldn't get here any sooner, but it is the grand opening *and* ladies' night, so I was expecting it to be longer than this."

While we waited in line, we talked among ourselves. Thankfully, it moved very quickly, and within fifteen minutes, we were inside.

"This shit is about to be lit! I'm so excited," Keyla said as she laced up her skates.

"Me too! I hope the DJ is good."

After making sure that my laces were tied just right, I stood and adjusted my fanny pack across my chest, then we skated over to one of the openings to the floor. Roller skating had been one of my favorite pastimes since I was a kid and something I continued to do as an adult. I'd been looking forward to tonight all week.

There was already a nice amount of people out there showcasing their skills, or lack thereof. As soon as there was an opening, we joined them, going to the middle of the floor. When my skates hit the smooth surface, I felt right at home. After going around a few times, I was comfortable enough to move a little closer to the outside.

"You ready to move out a little bit," I shouted over the music. Keyla nodded and followed me.

As I was getting into a groove, "Who Do You Love" by Bernard Wright blared through the speakers. That was one of my favorite old-school songs. By the time the song ended, I felt amazing. Just like dancing, roller skating made me feel free. The DJ was playing hits from the seventies, eighties, nineties, and today. Every time I was about to take a break, another song came on that I loved, and I ended up staying on the floor for a good forty-five minutes before finally taking a break. Keyla was right there with me.

Moving through the crowd, I went to the concession stand to buy two bottles of water, and Keyla went to the bathroom. When I got up to the counter, I felt a body pressed up against my backside, then saw male hands on the counter on either side of me. I angled my head, then looked up and behind me. He had gotten the attention of the cashier, and she addressed him instead of me.

"Yeah, let me get some nachos with extra cheese and jalapeños, a large Pepsi, and whatever she wants."

After he placed his order, he looked down at me and smiled. I shook my head, then turned to face the cashier.

"I'll have two bottled waters, please."

"Two? You got a nigga?"

"Fine time for you to ask, but no. It's for my cousin."

"Oh, just making sure. That's all you want, baby? You not hungry?" he asked.

"No, I'm good. Thanks."

The cashier rang him up, and after he paid, she handed me the bottles of water.

"Thanks again," I said as I began to skate away slowly.

"Hold up, shorty. You can't give me a few minutes after I just paid for you and your cousin's water?"

I looked at the water before focusing on him. Taking him in from head to toe, I observed his beige-colored skin, hazel eyes, and pink lips. Although he was wearing a Ralph Lauren baseball cap, his curly tresses were sticking out around the sides. He was tall, at least he looked to be with the skates on, and a little on the thin side. But he was handsome.

"I didn't ask you to buy our drinks, but I appreciate it," I told him.

"You're welcome. Can I get your name?"

"Bri."

"Well, Bri, I'm Torian. You not from around here, are you? I think I hear a little accent."

"No. I was born and raised in the A. Moved here not too long ago."

"I guess that explains why you don't look familiar. I would never forget such a pretty face."

Blushing a little, I replied, "Thank you."

"I won't hold you up, but umm, can I get your number?"

I touched my chin with my index finger and looked in the air, pretending as if I was giving his question some deep thought.

"Well, damn, shorty. I know I ain't no ugly nigga. You gotta think that hard?"

We both laughed. "I was just messing with you."

Taking my phone out of my fanny pack, I entered the passcode and handed it to him. After calling himself, he gave it back to me and took out his phone.

"Is it too soon to ask your last name?" he asked.

"For now, you can save me as Bri C."

He smiled and nodded while entering the information into his phone. When he looked up, he noticed that I had already put my phone away.

"You not gon' lock me in?"

"Hell naw, she not!" I heard Keyla's voice before I saw her, then she appeared next to me.

"Keyla, take yo' cockblockin' ass on, girl!" Torian shouted.

"You think I'm about to let your diseased-dick ass talk to my cousin? Let's go, Bri!"

She looped her arm through mine, and we rolled away. Once we were far enough away from Torian, we stopped and leaned against the half wall that separated the skating floor.

"Umm, so what that about?" I asked her, handing her one of the waters.

"Girl, Torian is a nasty nigga. He went to Howard and is from D.C. Fine as fuck but will stick his dick in anything moving, and don't believe in wrapping his shit up either. Nigga got six kids, and three of them are the same age. These thirsty ass bitches be giving it up, too."

"Well, damn! Let me block his number," I said, taking my phone out. "I'm glad you came along and stopped that train wreck."

"And it was surely about to be a wreck. Eww, I can't believe his ass. As soon as he saw an unfamiliar face, he couldn't wait to pounce." She shook her head in disgust.

"That's done," I affirmed after blocking his number.

We stayed there, people-watching and talking, while we finished drinking our waters. I tossed my empty bottle in the nearest recycle bin, and, as if on cue, one of our jams came on.

"Oh my God, Key! Do you remember our routine?" I asked as the DJ blending in "Elevators (Me & You)" by OutKast.

When we were fourteen or fifteen, not long after Keyla had come to live with us, we entered a skating contest at a local rink in Atlanta. The routine we made up to that song won us three hundred dollars.

"Hell yeah, I remember it. I ain't so sure I can still do it."

"Let's try!" I grabbed her hand and dragged her to the floor.

When the song came out, we were only ten or eleven years old, but our fathers, who were brothers, were huge OutKast fans, so we couldn't help but become fans as well. Not to mention they were from the A. As I got older, I had the biggest crush on André 3000. I found his quirkiness sexy when most thought he was weird. Hell, I still do.

Keyla and I fell in sync with each other. There were some parts of the routine that I remembered and some that she remembered. We followed each other's lead when our memory failed us. However, anyone watching would have thought that we'd put that routine together recently and been practicing for weeks. We were heavy in our zone as the DJ transitioned into "Turn the Lights Down Low" by Bob Marley featuring Lauryn Hill. I slowed down a bit and was about to do a turn so I could skate backward. However, I was unable to because of the hands around my waist.

Normally, I would have tried to get out of the grasp of some random stranger, but for some reason, being in his arms felt... right. Whoever it was smelled heavenly. The cologne he was wearing mixed well with his natural scent. As we glided along, my hands covered his, and our bodies moved in sync. I was anxious to see if his face matched the energy I felt radiated from his body. When he finally released my waist and took one of my hands to spin me around, I was able to catch a glimpse of his face. *Oh my Jesus!*

2

RASHAAD HANES

It was the night of our grand opening, and the line to get into Roll Bounce Love was wrapped around the building. I first had the idea to open a skating rink about four years ago. Skating had always been my passion, and I wanted to bring it to the forefront again like it was in the seventies and eighties. Initially, it was just a passing thought that I didn't know how to make a reality.

However, I shared the idea with my uncle Abe, and he was so excited about it he wanted to be partners. The more research we did, the more I started to believe it could happen. When I mentioned it to my younger brother and sister, Rashawn and Rasheeda, they wanted in on it as well, so we formed a four-way partnership.

My siblings and I worked at our father's construction company, Hanes Construction, since we were in high school. After Rashawn and I graduated from high school, a year apart, we both went to trade school and then followed that up with earning an associate's degree in business. It wasn't until then that our father hired us full time.

Rasheeda's work with Hanes Construction was on the management side because she had no desire to be in the field. She ended up getting a bachelor's degree in business from Howard University while continuing her job training in the office. When our father retired, naturally, the three of us were set to take over. However, he told us that he planned to work at least eight to ten more years and encouraged us to move forward with our plans for the skating rink.

Then my uncle passed away unexpectedly in his sleep. It had been almost a year, but my entire family was still in shock. He was the youngest of all six of my mother's siblings and, at the age of forty-one, the first one to die. Abraham Billard was single with no children and named me, Rashawn, and Rasheeda as the beneficiaries of a pretty hefty life insurance policy. This caused a huge rift in our family because we had several cousins that were angry that Uncle Abe left so much to us. They must have forgotten that my mother and father raised him from the age of twelve and put him through college.

My grandparents were both notorious chain smokers. My mother said that they were always made fun of growing up because their clothes reeked of cigarette smoke. She and my father began dating right out of high school, and as soon they could afford to, they found a place and moved in together.

When they found out that my mother was pregnant with me, they were both nineteen and went to the courthouse to get married. Fourteen months later, Rashawn came along, then four years after that, Rasheeda was born. By that time, my mother's relationship with her parents was strained because they wouldn't respect my parents' request for them to not smoke around us.

Right after my mother found out she was pregnant with Rasheeda, both her parents found out that they had stage four lung cancer. They died within months of each other. Uncle Abe was the only kid left at home, and my parents didn't hesitate to take him in and raise him as their own, even though there were only thirteen years between them.

Uncle Abe and I were only seven years apart while he and Rashawn were eight years. He was more like an older brother to us than an uncle and was our best friend. We felt his absence from our lives daily. For a while, we discontinued our plans for the skating rink, but my mother convinced us that her brother would want us to keep moving forward. After a few months of wallowing in grief, we did exactly that.

My siblings and I walked around and took in the vast space just before it was time to open. Our guests could enjoy old-school arcade games like Pac Man and Donkey Kong, Skee-Ball lanes, pool tables, and Super Shot basketball games along with roller skating. There would also be classic Black sitcoms playing on the televisions placed throughout, like *What's Happening, Different Strokes, The Jeffersons, Good Times,* and of course, *The Cosby Show* and *A Different World*. The concession stand would have the typical food that would be expected and would also be stocked with penny candy to add to the nostalgia.

We went back and forth about whether we would have theme nights but eventually decided against it. Well, sort of. We agreed that Friday night would be "Ladies' Night", and Sunday nights would be "Couples Skate", which would give us the flexibility to have themed parties a few times a month.

"Uncle Abe would be proud," Rasheeda said.

"He sure would," Rashawn replied.

"It's eight o'clock. Y'all ready to open the doors?" Barry, the head of security, asked.

"Let's do it!" we all said at the same time.

I had a feeling we'd be at capacity before the night was over, which was exactly what we wanted. I found a spot against the half wall that faced the main entrance and watched the people pour in. Rashawn and Rasheeda had wandered off to another part of the building.

About thirty minutes later, I was satisfied with how things were flowing. I moved away from the wall and made my rounds throughout the building, checking on each area and the employees. It was still early, but I was glad there were no fires that needed to be put out. We made sure that we hired qualified supervisors because we knew we couldn't be everywhere.

The first couple of hours flew by as I walked around and observed. My siblings and I crossed paths a few times but were rarely in the same place. The only thing missing was Uncle Abe. More than anything, I wished he could be there with us to celebrate.

Since everything was running smoothly, I decided to grab my skates and do a few spins on the floor. That was the only place I hadn't been, and I wanted to get a feel of what my patrons were experiencing. On the way to my office, I saw my brother and told him to get his skates. We met back up and made our way to one of the entrances to the floor.

As we waited for an opening to glide onto the floor, a vision of beauty passed me. She was with another woman, who was pretty as well, and they were mirroring each other's moves, doing a routine to "Elevators (Me & You)". As the song blared through the speakers, the one I had my eyes on was spitting the lyrics right along with André 3000 as she bodied the dance moves like she wasn't on eight wheels. There were a lot of great skaters in the building, but something about the way she moved was different. She was graceful yet edgy, smooth yet rough. I couldn't tear my eyes away from her if I wanted to as they passed us again. It was evident that she was an experienced skater, but I saw so much more.

"Damn!" Rashawn exclaimed as the two beauties passed us the second time. "Do you see what I see?"

I nodded as I tried not to lose sight of them.

"Which one you checking for because both of their asses fine as hell?"

"The one on the right," I told him.

"Good, because the one with the thick ass is calling me."

DJ CashFlo flawlessly blended in "Turn the Lights Down Low" by Bob Marley featuring Lauryn Hill, and I couldn't keep my distance any longer. As soon as she was close enough again, I grabbed her by the waist from behind and fell in sync with her movement. At first, her body tensed, but after a few seconds, she relaxed in my arms.

A minute or so passed, and I took one of her hands and spun her around. She was more beautiful close-up than she was from afar. The expression on her face told me that she was just as pleased with my appearance.

"Damn, you're beautiful," I said.

"Thank you," she replied, blessing me with a wide smile.

Suddenly, I saw a group of people gathering several feet away. I released the hold I had on the beautiful stranger and skated in the direction of the small crowd. Rashawn was right behind me, and Barry was already moving people out of the way. We were relieved to see that instead of a fight, it was a marriage proposal. The last thing we wanted to happen in our establishment, any time, but especially on the grand opening night, was a fight or any other kind of violence.

Once the excitement wore down, we introduced ourselves to the couple as the owners, and they asked if they could take a few pictures with us. We happily obliged, although my mind was elsewhere. After congratulating the couple, I moved through the sea of people, searching for the woman that would surely be in my dreams tonight. Just when I thought I spotted her, Rasheeda approached me.

"Shaad, is everything okay? I saw the crowd but couldn't get over there quick enough."

"Yeah, it's cool. Dude was just proposing to his girl. If something pops off, you need to make sure you stay as far away as possible. Me and Shawn got it, plus we have plenty of security. We can't have you inserting yourself and getting hurt," I told her.

"I own a third of this place, you know," she sassed.

"I don't give a damn. I will buy your ass out. Don't play with me, Rasheeda Faith Hanes."

"I would never sell, so you can calm all that nonsense down, and you ain't gotta call me by my full name," she said before walking away.

"Stay off the damn floor in your street shoes!" I shouted to her back.

I shook my head at her spoiled ass. Being the baby of three, with two brothers, not to mention the overbearing uncle that Abe was, I guess she can't help but be spoiled. My thoughts went back to the task at hand. I continued to look for the mysterious beauty and ran into Rashawn.

"Did you see where they went?" I asked him.

He shook his head. "I've been looking for about ten minutes. Seems like their asses disappeared."

I looked for about ten more minutes before I gave up. If it was meant to be, I'd see her again.

∽

THE FOLLOWING MORNING, I was awakened by my alarm clock at seven a.m., only getting a few hours of sleep. After a successful grand opening, RBL closed its doors at two a.m. Of course, as the owners, we had to stick around and make sure everything was cleaned, secured, and prepped for the following day.

By the time I got home, it was almost four in the morning. I was exhausted, but I had to pick up my daughter, Zara, from my parents' house. They were driving down to Virginia Beach to visit my aunt, who was having surgery and would need help around the house for about a week. If Zara didn't have school, I would've let her go because I could use a break from parenting.

After showering and throwing on some sweats and a long-sleeved T-shirt, I left my house and headed to pick up my angel. When I arrived, the garage door to my parents' house was open. As I approached the house, my father was coming out with a couple of small suitcases.

"You want me to get those for you, old man?" I joked.

He turned to look at me before placing the suitcases on the ground.

"Boy, who you calling old? I could pass for your brother, and you know it."

It was true. At the age of fifty-five, Raynard Hanes was in tip-top shape because he worked out regularly and still worked at construction sites on occasion.

"Yeah, my much-*older* brother," I teased.

"You must be still half asleep, coming to my house at this time of morning talking crazy."

After he put the suitcases in the trunk, I followed him inside.

"Daaddyy," Zara sang as she hopped out of the chair at the kitchen table.

"Hey, baby girl," I greeted as I picked her up. "Did you have fun with Gigi and Pop-Pop last night?"

"I did. We had pizza and ice cream and then watched *Princess and the Frog*. Pop-Pop fell asleep as soon as the movie started."

I gave her a tight hug, then kissed her forehead before putting her back on her feet.

"That's because Pop-Pop is an old man. Old men get tired real fast."

"Zanetta, you better get your son. If he calls me old one more time, I'm gon' take him to the backyard and show him how old I am," Dad fussed as he walked to the back of the house.

My mom shook her head as she leaned in to let me kiss her cheek. She was fifty-five as well and could pass for my sister. My father vowed to take care of her, and she hadn't worked outside of the home since Rasheeda was born. Their relationship was the epitome of Black Love in my opinion.

"Stop talking about my husband before you get jumped," Ma threatened.

I put my hands up in surrender. "Oh, it's like that? You would jump your firstborn child for him?"

"You darn right I would. That's my husband, and he always comes first, son."

I couldn't wait to have a woman in my life that had my back like that.

"I see how you are, Ma. Come on, Zee. Let's go before Gigi and Pop-Pop gang up on your daddy. Go get your bag."

She ran to the room she had at their house and returned seconds later with her duffel bag.

"I almost forgot. How was the grand opening?" Ma asked.

"It was great. Filled to capacity, no drama or fights, and one marriage proposal."

"Oh, wow! That's great, son. I knew it would be. Do you have everything squared away with a sitter for Zara tonight?"

"Sheeda agreed to watch her for me. It took some convincing because she wants to be at the rink as well, but she knows I don't have many choices. It's either y'all, Sheeda, or Shawn, and there was no way he'd miss the rink tonight. I'm not leaving my baby with nobody else."

"I know, son. I hate that we're leaving the weekend of your opening, but your aunt needs our help."

"It's cool, Ma. I understand. Y'all be careful driving and call or text me when you get there. Send my love to Aunt Rema."

My dad came from the back of the house, and we said our goodbyes. When Zara and I were settled in the car, I looked at the time and saw that we had forty minutes to get to her dance class.

Thankfully, Zara was already dressed for class as the Saturday morning traffic caused us to be pressed for time. Once we arrived, I picked her up and jogged inside. I put her down right outside of the door, helped her out of her light jacket and into her dance shoes, before kissing her forehead.

"Daddy will be right out here when you're done," I told her.

It was the first class of a new session at a new studio. The class she was taking was a mixture of everything from hip-hop dance to ballet, and I honestly couldn't wait to see how the instructor blended everything. I missed the open house last week because I was working on some last-minute details for the rink, and I was grateful that Rasheeda volunteered to come. I planned to stick around after class to meet her instructor, if there weren't too many other parents lingering around for the same reason.

There was a huge window on the back wall of the dance studio where Zara's class was held. Right outside of it, there was a room for spectators to watch. My stomach growled loudly, and I realized that I didn't have enough time to eat this morning. Instead of sitting, I went in search of a vending machine.

After turning a few corners, I found something better—a café. Once I purchased a green tea and blueberry muffin, I went back to the spectators' area to watch Zara's dance class. The other parents must have just dropped their kids off and left. I was the only parent there, which was cool because I didn't feel like having small talk. I took a bite of the muffin, then looked into the window. My heart almost jumped out of my chest when I saw the vision of beauty.

At the front of the studio, instructing the class, was the beautiful stranger from last night. I couldn't believe my eyes. *What were the odds?*

I watched her as she spoke to the six- and seven-year-old boys and girls. Although I couldn't hear anything she said, I could tell by her demeanor that she was good with kids.

Under the dim lights at the skating rink, I thought she was gorgeous, but under the bright lights of the studio, she was breathtaking. Her straight hair that went past her shoulders, was pulled back into a bun at the nape of her neck. She was wearing a leotard, and although she had a pair of leggings on over it, I was still able to admire her petite but curvy frame. She didn't have a typical dancer's body. Her skin was the color of rich cream, and maybe it was just me, but she had a glow radiating around her.

She must have felt me staring because she looked up. Our eyes connected, but her expression wasn't one of recognition, so I wasn't sure if she remembered me. It didn't matter, though, because she would damn sure know who I was as soon as class was over. For the next hour, my focus went back and forth between my baby girl and her fine ass dance instructor.

3

AUBRIELLE

"Okay, class. Great job today. Remember, we have a total of six weeks to prepare for the Groove Motion Fall Festival, and you all are gonna rock it. Don't forget to give your parents the permission slips, and I'll see you on Monday."

"Yaayy!" the entire class of six- and seven-year-old girls and boys cheered as they were released from dance class.

"Ms. Aubrielle, my water spilled on my permission slip. May I have another one, please?"

"Of course, Zara. Let me go grab one out of the office."

"Okay."

It was the first class of a new session, but I could already see that Zara was the most talented student in that group. I expected all of the kids to be talented because Groove Motion Dance School was one of the most prestigious in the area. All students had to audition and were carefully chosen by the owners and the board of directors.

Even among all of the other talent, Zara stood out. I'd definitely be moving her up a level after the festival. I'd have to chat with her parents to see how they felt about it. After grabbing a permission slip from my desk, I stepped out of my office to head back to the studio and froze when I saw Zara standing by the door with... *him*.

The fine ass stranger from the skating rink looked even better during the day. The butterflies that floated around my stomach when I saw his face last night returned, and I couldn't understand the pull he seemed to have on me. I had never experienced anything like it.

His skin was the color of milk chocolate and looked so smooth. He had a muscular build but was very lean, and the tattoos on his arms added a roughness to his appearance that had me thinking nasty thoughts. This morning, he had on a baseball hat, but I remembered that he had a low Caesar cut from last night. The minimal facial hair he sported gave him a youthful look, but I was hoping he was at least thirty.

"Hi," I said nervously when I finally stopped lusting over him and approached them.

"Hi. I'm Rashaad, Zara's dad," he responded, offering his hand.

"I'm Aubrielle—"

"Ms. Aubrielle," Zara corrected me.

"Yes, I'm Ms. Aubrielle Carson. Nice to meet you."

When he took my hand in his, my entire body went up in flames. I tried to pull away, but he tightened his grip, which caused me to look at him.

"You got away from me last night before I could shoot my shot."

"You remember me?"

"I would never forget a face, or aura, like yours. I know it sounds cliché, but you were the subject of my dreams this morning."

I smiled. "You're right. It's very cliché. How many times have you used that pick-up line?"

"It's cool if you don't believe me. I'm still gon' shoot my shot, though."

"Okay... shoot."

"Can I have—"

"Yes," came out of my mouth before he could finish his question.

That caused him to smirk as he released my hand and reached for his phone. After entering the code, he gave it to me, and I locked my number in.

"If I call this number, it's not gonna be Pizza Hut or some shit—"

"Daaddyy!" Zara scolded.

"My bad, Zee. Daddy's just trying to make sure Ms. Aubrielle gave me the right phone number."

"It's the right number," I assured him.

"Good. What time are you done today?"

"My last class ends at noon."

He nodded. "Okay, Ms. Aubrielle. I'm gonna text you so you'll have my number, and I'll be calling you this afternoon. Make sure you pick up."

As I watched him and Zara leave, I couldn't stop smiling if you paid me. Last night, when he touched me, I felt a jolt of electricity move through my body, spending some extra time at my neglected vagina. Although he was a complete stranger, there was something eerily familiar about him. I had no idea who he was, but I already felt comfortable around him. I'd surely be answering when he called.

FIVE HOURS LATER, I had made it to our empty house. Keyla was a registered nurse and was working a twelve-hour shift. I went straight to the bathroom, stripped off my clothes, and started the shower. When my phone rang with a number that I didn't have saved, I knew it was Rashaad. He'd sent me a text, just as he said he would, but I hadn't saved his number yet.

For two seconds, I contemplated letting it go to voicemail and calling him back when I finished my shower. However, I didn't want him to think I was curving him, and I was anxious as hell. So I answered.

"Hello?"

"Ms. Aubrielle?"

"That's me."

"Do I hear water running? Did I catch you at a bad time?"

"I just got home and was about to jump in the shower."

"Damn! I knew I should have FaceTimed you," he joked.

I laughed before saying, "I probably wouldn't have answered, but nice try."

"Well, I'm gonna let you take your shower and get comfortable."

"Okay. I'll call you back in about twenty minutes."

"I'll be waiting, beautiful."

We ended the call, and I took a quick but thorough shower. After putting on a pair of spandex shorts and a sports bra, I made and ate a peanut butter and jelly sandwich, then went to my room and got comfortable on my bed. Picking up my phone, I saved Rashaad's number before calling him back. The phone only rang once before he picked up, and as soon as I heard his voice, the nerves I felt disappeared.

"You only had about five more minutes before I started blowing you up," he answered.

"I'm sorry. I had to make myself a peanut butter and jelly sandwich."

"Peanut butter and jelly? No shit?"

"Yep! That's my go-to."

"That's wild."

"What's so wild about a PB&J sandwich?"

"I try to eat healthy for the most part. I'm not a health fanatic, but I do watch what I put in my body most of the time. But peanut butter and jelly sandwiches are my one weakness. I have to be careful, or I'd eat one every day."

"Really? That's a cute coincidence. I can't eat them like that. It would go straight to my hips."

"Ain't nothing wrong with hips. Just more to hold on to."

His forwardness had me raising my eyebrows in surprise, but I liked it. When I didn't respond, he must have thought I was offended by his comment and somewhat apologized.

"My bad, beautiful. I know I'm coming on strong, but last night I felt something when my eyes landed on you. The feeling only got stronger when my hands gripped your waist. I'm a straightforward kinda nigga, and I don't have a problem expressing myself. I don't know what it is about you, but I plan to find out if you let me."

"I'd like that, Rashaad. Tell me what I need to know about you. I already feel like you may be a little too good to be true."

He chuckled a bit before asking, "What do you wanna know?"

"Eventually, everything, but for now, whatever you feel comfortable sharing."

There was a brief moment of silence, and I wasn't sure how to perceive that. *Did he not want to tell me about himself, or was he trying to decide what he wanted me to know?* When he finally spoke, I felt a sense of relief.

"I have a feeling it won't be long before you know everything there is to know about me. But there is one thing I want to tell you up front."

"What's that?"

"You already know that Zara is my daughter."

"Yeah."

"I assume you don't have any issues with dating a man with a child."

"I've never dated a man with children, but I'm not opposed it."

"That's good to know. Several months ago, Carmen, Zara's mother, decided she didn't want to be a mother anymore, signed over her parental rights, and left. Since then, I've been adjusting to single fatherhood."

"Wow," was all I could say to that. I wasn't expecting that. I didn't even have children, and I couldn't imagine giving up all my rights to my child.

"Yeah, it sucks, but it is what it is. I'm grateful that my family helps me out a lot. Other than that, I'm not crazy, I've never been arrested, and I don't nor have I ever had any sexually transmitted diseases. I love my daughter more than life, and she's my everything. I'm not looking for anyone to be a mother to her, but whoever I decide to spend the rest of my life with has to have a strong connection with my baby girl."

"That's understandable. I've only had a couple of interactions with Zara, but she seems like an amazing little girl."

"She is, and I'm glad you recognize that already. I'm a man who is led by his spirit, and my spirit tells me that you're someone special."

"Really? What else does your spirit tell you about me?"

"That you've been hurt before, but you haven't given up on love. Your heart is open as long as it's the right man."

"Continue."

"Since you're a dance instructor, I already know that you're a creative and sensitive about your shit. You enjoy being independent, but you have no problem letting your man lead. And you're a people person but enjoy spending time alone just as much."

This nigga read me like a book.

"Are you sure you're not some kind of crazy mind reader or something? You just described me to a tee. How did you do that?"

"My spirit tells me what I need to know. I haven't always listened, and nine times out of ten, I regretted it later. The older I get, the more obedient I've become."

"And exactly how old are you?"

"I just turned thirty-five last month, on August sixth."

"Really? My birthday is August sixteenth, and I turned thirty-four."

"Happy belated birthday, beautiful."

"You too, handsome."

"Anything else you want to know about me will have to wait," he told me. "But I do have a question for you."

"Shoot."

"I know D.C. is big, but how come I've never seen you before?"

"Probably because I've only lived here for six months. I'm from Atlanta."

"Oh, so that *is* an accent I hear. It's not too strong, though. What made you move to D.C.?"

"Let's just say I needed a change and leave it at that," I told him.

"I sense you have a story to tell, but if you're not ready to share, I understand. How long you been skating?"

"As long as I can remember. Skating is my second passion after dance. Growing up, me and my cousin Keyla spent almost every weekend at the skating rink. When she went away to school and I started at Emory, I didn't go as often. In the last couple of years, I've been going any time my schedule permitted with my girl Laniyah. I was so excited when Keyla told me about Roll Bounce Love."

"Last night, I had my eyes on you for a while before I approached you," he admitted. "I could tell you weren't an amateur."

"Well, I'm not a professional either, but I do okay. I'm guessing you enjoy skating, too."

"I do, and I'm glad we have that in common. So, the girl with you last night, was that Keyla?"

"Yeah, why?"

"My brother was checking her out. When I tell him that I connected with you, he may want you to hook them up."

"I might be able to do that. Let me see how things between us pan out first."

"I guess I can tell him to wait for her call," he responded.

"You're mighty confident, Mr. Hanes."

"You can be when you know what you bring to the table."

"I hear you."

There was a stretch of silence where neither of us spoke, and surprisingly, it wasn't awkward at all. I ended up being the one to speak again.

"You tired of talking to me already?"

"Hell, naw. I could listen to your sexy ass voice all day and night. I'm intrigued by you and how you make me feel after only two brief encounters and one phone conversation."

"How do I make you feel?"

"It's hard to explain. The feeling is unfamiliar and familiar all wrapped up in one. Does that make sense?"

"Not really," I said with a laugh, although I knew exactly what he meant because I felt the same way.

"Let me see if I can explain it." He paused. "Being around you and hearing your voice brings me a sense of peace. Something feels familiar about you like I knew you in a past life or something, but I've never felt any of this before, so it's unfamiliar."

This man was... overwhelming but in a good way. I was so taken by his words I couldn't respond.

"That's the best way that I can explain it. Look, I know I'm a lot. I don't have time for games. I'm dating with a purpose. I want friendship, commitment, loyalty, love, and ultimately marriage. I don't want to scare you away before you have a chance to get to know the man I am, but if that's not the shit you on, let a nigga know now."

"When you wrapped your arms around my waist last night, it felt right. I knew then that there was something different about you. I've never met a man that was so confident about what he wanted from a woman. I love it, and I would like to see where this goes."

"Good, because I was gon' stalk your ass until you agreed to see this through, anyway. Now that's not necessary." He chuckled, but I could sense that he was serious as well.

"I thought you said you weren't crazy. That sounds a little crazy."

"Naw, I'm just messing with you. You just made my day, beautiful."

We ended up staying on the phone for an hour and a half, discussing just about everything, including our sexual history. Both of us had been tested within the last four months, and neither of us had been sexually active for at least six months. I was blown away by the things we had in common. It was like the universe was preparing us for each other.

He shared that his parents got married young and raised him, his younger brother and sister, and his uncle to value love and relationships. However, none of them had been fortunate in that department. I also hadn't had much luck finding my forever love, even though my parents set a fantastic example.

It was crazy how similar our upbringing was, as my parents married young and were still married. Even the part about his parents raising his uncle was similar to my parents raising Keyla. I was almost brought to tears when he talked about his uncle passing away. The emotion in his voice was evident, and I could tell that they were extremely close.

"I wish we could talk longer, but I have to get to work. You mind if I call you when I get a break?" he said suddenly.

"What do you do?"

"I just started a job at this new place that opened up."

Okay, that was pretty vague.

Sensing he didn't want to share more than that, I said, "Oh, okay. Well, I won't be doing anything but binge-watching something on Netflix. Feel free to call on your break."

"Cool. I'll call you later on."

"Sounds good."

The call ended, and I remained in the same position, laying on my bed with my phone in my hand, thinking about the conversation I'd just had with Rashaad. He was unlike any man I'd ever dated, which was probably a good thing since they all ended up being assholes. His forwardness, confidence, and good looks all wrapped up in one man... *whew*! There is no way I'd be able to resist him.

Unlocking my phone, I went to the Instagram app and searched his full name on the explore page. Maybe there would be some clues about what he did for a living since he didn't seem to want to share. Three people came up, and the third one was a match. The most recent picture that he'd posted was in front of Roll Bounce Love with Zara. The caption read, "Uncle Abe, we did it." I had no clue what that meant, but he tagged the roller rink's page, so I went there to continue snooping.

I swiped to the bottom of the page to find the first picture that was posted. It was of a building that looked like the skating rink without the finishing touches. As I moved through each one, it was all coming together. By the time I got to the most recent picture that was posted, I realized that Rashaad and his siblings were the owners of the skating rink.

"Wow!"

My nosy ass wasn't satisfied with that tidbit of information, so I decided to google his name plus the name of the rink, and a few articles that led up to the grand opening confirmed my suspicions.

"But why didn't he tell me?"

Until then, I had no plans to go out, but I was suddenly in the mood for another night of skating.

4

RASHAAD

I was excited to see that Roll Bounce Love was once again filled to capacity on the second night of business. Some of the same faces from the previous night were back, along with some that didn't make the grand opening. As I made my rounds to each area of the rink, everyone seemed to be having a great time.

"Hey, Rashaad," I heard as I exited the arcade and headed back toward the skate floor.

When I looked to my left, I saw that it was Joanna, a woman I'd been messing around with most recently, although I hadn't hooked up with her in several months.

"Wassup, Jo? Long time no see," I said as I continued walking.

"Not because I haven't tried. Did you block my number or something?"

"Naw, of course not. I wouldn't do you like that, but I did get a new phone and a new number several months ago. Maybe your number got lost in the transition."

"Okay, let me get your new number. Maybe we can get together soon."

I patted my pockets as if I was looking for my phone, which I knew was locked in my office.

"Damn! My phone must be in my office, and I don't have my number memorized."

"That's cool. I'll get it from you later."

I nodded, surprised that she fell for that. I didn't get a new phone. I'd just been ignoring her calls. After Carmen left, I was focused on my daughter's mental health. Between that and opening up RBL, I had enough on my plate and didn't feel like dealing with Joanna or any other woman.

I leaned against the half wall around the skating floor and watched the patrons. Because of the music and chatter of the crowd, Joanna was standing fairly close to me to avoid shouting. However, when her breasts unnecessarily brushed up against my arm, I looked down at her, and she had a flirty smile on her face.

"So how you been?" she asked.

"Busy… very busy."

"Oh, yeah. This *is* your establishment, huh?"

She said that shit like she'd just remembered it. I nodded and focused on the crowd, hoping Joanna would take note of my disinterest. As I watched everyone passing by, I saw someone that looked like Aubrielle.

"It's nice. So, umm, I heard you're *single*, single, meaning she's no longer living with you. Maybe it's time for us to try to have something real."

Joanna knew about my situation with Carmen but never believed that we weren't still sleeping together. It was mighty funny how that didn't stop her from giving me the pussy, though. Just as I was about to respond to her suggestion, the woman came back around, and all I could do was smile.

"I'm not single, but you take care. I'm sure I'll be seeing you around."

I quickly walked away, purposely losing Joanna in the crowd. In my office, I sat in the chair behind my desk and grabbed the bag where I kept my skates. As I left my office with my skates on, I bumped into my brother.

"Where you rushing off to?" he asked.

"Ole girl from last night is here.

"Oh, word? Is her girl with her."

"I'm not sure. I didn't see her, though."

"Cool."

When I got back to the floor, I anxiously waited at one of the openings for Aubrielle to appear. When I saw her, I let her pass before gliding on and falling in line behind her. I admired the way her body moved to the beat of "Give it 2 You" by Da Brat. I'd only had the pleasure of seeing her on skates once before, but she seemed to become one with the music. I was sure that had something to do with her experience as a dancer. As the DJ slowed the music and "Falsetto" by The Dream came on, I caught up to her and gripped her waist the same way I did the night before.

"This looks nothing like binge-watching Netflix," I said with my mouth close to her ear as my hands eased around her waist.

"Shit, Rashaad. You scared me," she fussed but relaxed in my arms.

I guided her to the center of the floor, where couples generally went to slow-skate.

"Why didn't you tell me you were coming?" I asked once we'd gotten into a groove.

"Why didn't you tell me you owned this place?"

"Touché."

We skated for a little while in silence before I spoke again.

"I was gonna mention it... eventually."

"You told me damn near your whole life story, but you couldn't tell me that you and your siblings owned this spot. Let me guess! Did you want to feel me out a little more to make sure I wasn't a gold digger or some shit?"

I shrugged my shoulders, slightly embarrassed by her quick assessment.

"You mean to tell me your spirit didn't tell you that I don't care about shit like that? I don't need anything from you, Rashaad. If that's the kind of woman you think I am, then we don't have to take this any further. You can delete my number."

She tried to pull away from me, but I pulled her against my chest, and we continued to move to the music.

"My bad, Aubrielle. Occasionally, I overthink things, and my brain was telling me to pump the brakes."

"Well, listen to your brain because, just like you, I don't have time for games. You talked all that shit, and clearly that's all it was."

"It wasn't, baby, I swear. It was the logical side of me being cautious. The way I'm feeling about you is foreign to me, and I'm trying to get a handle on this shit. I've barely known you for twenty-four hours, and this is only the third time I've laid eyes on you, but I already feel like you're mine."

"You think I'm that easy?" she asked, curling her lips and raising her eyebrows as she waited for me to reply.

Instead of answering her, I spun her around and guided her off the floor and toward my office. We maneuvered our way through the crowd, with me holding her hand and pulling her along. When I unlocked the door, I felt some resistance when I tried to go inside.

"What are you doing?" she asked when I turned to face her.

"I'm trying to have a conversation with you without the distractions."

She looked as if she was thinking about it and then took her phone out of her fanny pack. I watched as she pressed a bunch of keys before sliding it back inside.

"I had to tell my cousin where I was just in case your ass is really crazy."

Shaking my head, I chuckled at her silly ass before I moved back to allow her inside. Closing and locking the door behind me, I turned around to see her sitting on the edge of my desk with her skates dangling just above the floor.

Moving to the other side of my desk, I sat down and removed my skates, replacing them with my shoes, then went back around and stood in between Aubrielle's legs.

"I told you I'm not crazy."

"I'll be the judge of that."

I loved that she still had a sense of humor about this.

"I never thought you were on bullshit. I just—"

"It's fine. I get it."

"It's not fine. The vibes I get from you are all positive. What I'm feeling is crazy as hell, and I was trying to make it make sense," I admitted. "Don't you feel the connection between us, or is this one-sided?"

Just by how her breathing hiked when I was near her let me know that she was feeling me.

"It's not one-sided. I feel it, too. But I don't—"

Before she could finish her sentence, my mouth covered hers with a soft kiss. Her lips felt like satin, and right away, I knew that kissing her would become one of my favorite things to do. When I pulled away, our eyes met, and I searched for any signs of rejection in hers. Thankfully, I saw none, giving me the green light to do it again.

This time, within seconds of our lips connecting, I felt her tongue requesting entrance into my mouth while her arms went around my neck. I allowed her access, and our tongues united in an anxious frenzy. Aubrielle tasted sweet, like she'd just finished eating a strawberry Jolly Rancher. My mind began to wonder what she might taste like between her thighs, causing my dick to stiffen.

Taking a chance, I pushed her back onto the desk, positioning my dick over her mound. We continued to kiss like familiar lovers as I began to grind against her. Even though she still had on her heavy skates, she lifted her legs around my waist, locking her ankles.

The shirt she was wearing was cropped and stopped at the middle of her abdomen. In her current position, her entire stomach was exposed, giving me easy access to her breasts. I leaned to the side, slid my hand underneath her shirt, and palmed her breast.

I gave it a gentle squeeze, then used my thumb to softly graze her hard nipple through her bra, but that wasn't enough. I wanted to feel her skin, so I tugged at the lace, and her breast popped out from the covering. Her nipple felt like pebbles and hardened even more under my touch. With the strong urge to tease it with my tongue, I finally tore my mouth away from hers and smothered her breast.

"Sss," she hissed upon contact.

As I flicked my tongue across one nipple, I used my free hand to massage the other. Aubrielle began to moan and used her skate-ladened feet to apply more pressure between us. We both had been sexually deprived for months, and although I was certain she was wetter than Niagara Falls, the last time I busted a nut from dry-humping, I was twelve years old. Right now, I was close to letting one blow.

To relieve the pressure on my dick, I stood upright, causing Aubrielle's legs to fall to the side and the skates to crash into the back of my desk. I could feel her eyes on me, and as my hand groped her pussy through the thin leggings, I returned her glare. She was so wet that her juices had seeped through and had her soaked.

"Damn, baby. All this juice for me?"

She had the nerve to hide her face with her hands as she blushed with embarrassment. Using my other hand, I pulled hers away from her face and smirked.

"Don't be embarrassed, baby. You want this dick, huh?"

"Maybe."

"Maybe my ass. This wet ass pussy is telling a different story."

She replied by blushing again but didn't say anything.

"This ain't how I imagined our first time together, so I can't give you this dick right now."

The disappointment in her face amused me. I was grateful that we discussed our sexual history and exchanged our latest STD test results earlier that day. If we hadn't, I wouldn't be able to do what I had in mind.

"Chill, baby. I'm gon' still take care of you."

My hands went to the waistband of her leggings, and when I began to pull them down, along with her lace panties, she lifted her hips a little to assist me. When her bare pussy was uncovered and I saw her nectar glistening, I looked up to the heavens and thanked God Almighty for the blessing that was before me.

Her sweet aroma hit my nostrils, beckoning me and making my mouth water. Pushing the suddenly annoying material down to her ankles, I got on my knees and maneuvered my body in between her legs. Pulling her beyond the edge of the desk so that her ass was hanging off, I submerged my face into the already-flowing dam.

"Fucckkk!" she screamed at the top of her lungs.

Thank God the music was loud enough to camouflage her screams. They were just the ammunition I needed to snatch her soul. My tongue touched every nook and cranny of her pussy, neglecting nothing. When I pushed it deep inside her hole and pressed the firmness of my nose against her clit, her hands went to the back of my head. She applied so much pressure that if I didn't know what I was doing, I would have suffocated.

"Oh my God, Rashaaaaddd! Shit! I'm 'bout to—"

The levy broke before she could finish, and I lapped that shit up like a dehydrated dog. I felt her trying to push me away, but the way we were positioned, and the fact that she still had her skates on, made that impossible. I continued my tongue lashing until she came again and was begging me to stop.

When I removed my face from her haven and lifted her legs over my head, both of us were out of breath. As we stared each other down, I helped her up and carefully lifted her from the desk. She must have forgotten about the skates on her feet, not to mention her legs may have been a little weak. After almost losing her balance, she held on to me as she bent over to pull up her panties and leggings. I noticed the puddle of liquid she left behind and knowing where it came from had my semi-hard dick becoming rock hard again.

"Baby, you made sure to leave your mark," I teased.

She turned to see what I was talking about and gasped before burying her face in my chest.

"Oh my God! I'm so embarrassed."

Embracing her, I kissed the topped of her head before assuring her that there was nothing to be embarrassed about. Releasing her, I walked around to the other side of my desk and retrieved some wipes from one of the drawers. She reached for them, and I snatched them away, then cleaned up her little mess.

"Do I look okay?" she asked as we approached the door.

"If you're asking if you look like you just came twice all over my face, no."

"Seriously, Rashaad. We've been in here a long time. I don't want to look like—"

"I'm just playing with your pretty ass. You look fine. You're glowing even more than you were before."

Rolling her eyes, she reached for the doorknob, and I stopped her.

"We good?" I asked.

Instead of responding with words, she put both of her hands on my cheeks and pulled me into a kiss. No tongue action this time. Simply a long, lingering, full-lipped peck that I enjoyed just as much.

"After what you just did to me, we're great."

5

AUBRIELLE

Sunday was my lazy day and always had been. Even when I worked at the studio in Atlanta, it was closed on Sundays. Like most people, I used the day to catch up on sleep, laundry, and TV shows. Since I moved to D.C., Sunday was one of the days that I set aside to call my parents and my friend Laniyah; Wednesday was the other. However, this particular Sunday, I had plans, so I had to make my phone calls early.

"Bri, you're up early. Is everything okay?" my mother, Aubrey, said when she answered the phone.

"Yes, Ma, everything is fine. I have a breakfast date this morning, and I'm not sure how the rest of my day will go, so I decided to call you before I left."

"A breakfast date? That's different. Tell me about this young man, and you're on speaker, so your father is listening."

"Hey, Daddy."

"Good morning, baby girl. Tell me about this nigga. He must be special if he got you outta bed this early."

Leave it up to Brighton Carson to never hold his tongue and always speak his mind.

"He seems pretty special. He and his siblings just opened up a skating rink. The grand opening was Friday night, and that's kinda where we met."

"How do you *kinda* meet someone?" Ma asked.

"We skated together for a bit but didn't exchange names or numbers. Turns out, his daughter is in one of my dance classes," I explained.

"Aw, shit! He got kids? I can tell you right now this ain't gon' work, Bri," came from my dad.

"Daddy, he doesn't have kids. He has one six-year-old daughter."

"You better be careful with that one. You know how men are with the mothers of their children," my mother warned.

"I don't think it'll be a problem. Anyway, I just wanted to call you guys so you won't be wondering why you didn't hear from me today. I about to call Niyah right quick so I can finish getting ready."

"Okay, Bri. We'll talk to you later. I can't wait to hear how this date goes. Call me later if you feel up to it."

"I will, Ma. Love you guys."

"We love you, too," they both sang.

Ending the call with my parents, I immediately found Laniyah's contact information and selected it. I wasn't sure she'd answer, because, like me, she was not an early riser.

"Bri, did something happen?" she said when she picked up.

"Dang, you sound like Aubrey and Brighton. Nothing happened. I'm just making my phone calls early today."

"Well, friend, you gon' have to call me back when I'm coherent. It's too early."

"Niyah, it's almost nine o'clock. It's not that early."

"It is for me. You know I keep late hours."

Laniyah was a stripper. We met and became close friends when she enrolled in one of my pole dancing sessions.

"I have a breakfast date, and—"

"You have a breakfast date? Well, it's about damn time you moved on from Damon's ass and found you another nigga."

"First of all, I moved on from Damon when I left his ass. Actually, before that. Me not dating had nothing to do with him."

"Okay, friend, if you say so. Tell me about him."

"We just met a couple of nights ago, but I already like him more than I want to admit. I got a good feeling about him."

"You had a good feeling about Damon, too, and look how that turned out."

"Niyah, I'd appreciate it if you'd stopped bringing him up. As a matter of fact, I need to get off this phone before I'm late. I'll talk to you later."

"Wait!" I heard her shout as I ended the call.

Laniyah was cool for the most part, but sometimes she could be negative, and that shit was annoying. I was sure I'd be receiving a text from her within the next few minutes apologizing and telling me to call her when I had time. After plugging my phone into the charger, I took a shower and dressed in a pair of black jeans and a denim button-down shirt.

"You're up and dressed this early on a Sunday?" Keyla said when I walked out of my room.

"I sure am. I have a breakfast date with Rashaad. The rink is open from two to midnight on Sundays, and he has to be there most of the day."

I hadn't seen much of Keyla since Friday night. I'd gone to the skating rink alone last night because she was tired from working a long shift at the hospital. The only thing she knew was that he owned the skating rink and his daughter was one of my students.

"You must really like him because I know how you are about your Sundays."

"Key, I do like him, too much for only knowing him a couple of days. He's not like anybody I've ever dated."

"That's a good thing since it didn't work out with none of those lame ass niggas. Who cares how long it's been? Just go with the flow. Now, spill the beans, Bri. What's so different about him?"

"Everything."

"Cousin, can you be more specific?"

"Well, to start, he has full custody of his daughter and is raising her alone with the help of his family. Now you know it takes a special kinda man to do that."

"Facts."

"And he's so... spiritually grounded."

"Oh, like he goes to church?" Keyla asked.

"No, I mean, he may go to church, but he didn't mention it. That's not what I meant by spiritually grounded. To use his words, he is a man that is led by his spirit."

"Damn, that's kinda deep."

"Ain't it? He's also very straightforward and verbally expressive. And guess what he called me?"

"What?"

"Elle," I said and waited for her reaction.

"Stop playing! He called you Elle?" I nodded. "Bri, he may be the one."

I shrugged my shoulders, brushing off her comment, even though I briefly had the same thought.

"I've never dated a man that was so open with his feelings. It's somewhat refreshing. I seriously have to remind myself to slow down because I can see myself falling for him."

"Why do you need to slow down? You're grown as hell and have nothing to lose. I know after dealing with Damon's fuck boy ass and the fuck boys before him, you may want to be guarded. Don't let your past relationships keep you from fully embracing the possibilities of what you could have with Rashaad."

"Look at you, giving what sounds like good relationship advice."

"It is good, and I'm serious, Bri. I've dealt with my share of fuck boys, too. Each time a relationship doesn't work out, I promise myself not to make the next man suffer because of the mistakes of the ones before him. It just ain't fair, and I'm not trying to miss out on something great because I keep picking assholes."

"I feel you, cousin, and I completely agree with you. My heart is open and ready to find my forever. I haven't known him for very long and..." I paused as I debated whether or not I wanted to tell her about the night before.

"And what?"

"Well, you know how I am about having sex too soon."

"Bri, did you give that man some pussy already?"

"Well, kind of."

"What! Oh my God! I was kidding! Are you serious? I need details. What do you mean 'kind of'? How do you 'kind of' give up the pussy? Either you did, or you didn't," Keyla rambled on a mile a minute, not giving me a chance to reply.

"He ate my pussy on his desk in his office," I blurted out.

Her eyes got as big as saucers, and her mouth was open wide with shock. By society's standards, I would be considered a late bloomer, and even after I lost my virginity, at twenty-one, I was still very selective with who I gave my body to. My body count was low, and I had never considered having sex with someone I'd known for such a short time. Keyla knew that about me, so I understood her surprise.

"Key, don't look at me like that," I continued when she didn't say anything. "This man got me acting *all outta character*. What is wrong with me? I didn't even try to stop him... *like at all*. I was a willing participant, and it was sooooo good."

"Girl, I ain't judging. It's about time you loosened up and lived a little. I can't wait until you let him blow your back out."

"Shit, I probably would've let him last night had he tried. I was sitting on his desk, and he stood between my legs. When we kissed..." I closed my eyes and shook my head as I thought back to the moment our lips touched. "It was magical. My pussy instantly got wet. I'm telling you, the only reason we didn't have sex was because he didn't want our first time to be in his office on his desk. Cousin, I was ready to bust it wide open for that nigga."

"Wow! I never thought I'd see the day. He's different, Bri. This," she waved her hand around me, "is different. A good different. All I can say is, if Rashaad is letting his spirit guide him, you should do the same."

I didn't reply to her as I headed for the door, but I heard every word she said. Right before I stepped outside, I remembered something.

"Oh, I gave him your number to give to his brother," I said before closing the door behind me.

∼

I THOUGHT about Keyla's last words as I drove to Florida Avenue Grill, where Rashaad and I were meeting for breakfast. I wasn't nearly as spiritually grounded as Rashaad seemed to be, but I knew when to listen to my gut. So far, it was quiet and giving me the all clear to free fall into whatever this was becoming between us. I thought back to last night when he walked me to my car.

I leaned against it, and he trapped me between his arms. He pressed his body against mine, and our faces were so close that our noses were touching. I could smell my scent on his face, and the fact that he hadn't washed it off turned me on a little bit. Well, a lot. The way he looked into my eyes was so intense. It felt like he was staring into my soul.

When our lips met, he kissed me as if he already missed me. Our tongues became so intertwined that I couldn't distinguish mine from his, and I enjoyed the taste of my flavor that lingered on his. People were walking by, several of them making comments, but none of that seemed to matter. After several minutes, he pulled away, and I could tell that it was a struggle.

"My dick is hard as fuck right now. I don't think I've ever gotten this hard from kissing."

I almost told him how wet my pussy was, but instead, I said, "I wish I could take care of that for you, but you have to get back to work."

"Elle, don't play with me."

"Elle?"

Hearing him call me by that name sent chills down my spine. It had been years since I'd heard it.

"Yeah," he replied before pecking my lips. "You mind if I call you Elle? It means sunray or shining light. I could use some light in my life and feel like you're exactly what I need."

"The only person that's ever called me that is my grandfather. We were super close before he died when I was twelve."

"I'm sorry, baby. I didn't mean—" he began.

"No, no. It's fine if you call me that. It just caught me by surprise."

"You sure?"

"I'm positive."

"Cool. I think my dick went down, so I should probably take my ass inside before you get my mans all riled up again."

"Oh, so all that was my fault?"

"Most definitely. Let's meet for breakfast tomorrow. I gotta be here for most of the day, and I wanna see you."

"Sundays are usually my lazy day, but for you, I can do breakfast."

He smiled and kissed me again. "I'll text you the details."

Just thinking back to that moment had me moist between the legs. Thankfully, I'd arrived at my destination, and I had something else to focus on. Shaking off the memories of the night before, I found a place to park and sent Rashaad a text to find out his location. He was already inside and seated. When I walked inside the cozy restaurant, the aroma of breakfast foods caused my stomach to growl and my mouth to water. I looked around for Rashaad and spotted him at a table in the back corner.

The smile on his face when he noticed me coming toward him made me feel all warm and fuzzy inside. He genuinely looked happy to see me. By the time I reached the table, he was on his feet. I thought he was about to pull out my chair, but instead, he pulled me into a hug that I could have remained in forever. When he buried his face in my neck and brushed his lips across my skin, my already-damp panties became even more so. Finally, he let me go and pulled out my chair.

After I was comfortably seated, he went back to his seat, and as soon as he sat down, he reached across the table to hold my hands. Not saying a word, he stared at me, making me blush.

"Why are you looking at me like that?" I asked.

"Because you're so beautiful. When I looked up and saw you, there was a glow around you. You truly are a ray of light."

I was sure my face was bright red at that point. I smiled and lowered my head, but he used his index finger to lift it back up.

"You may as well get used to me complimenting you. I can't help myself."

"Thank you," was all I could think of to say. "What's good here? I've never been."

"The best meal in this place right now is between your legs, but that ain't on the menu. The food here is good, though."

He released my hands and picked up the menus, passing me one of them. I was briefly stunned by his words and sat staring at him for a moment. Shaking the nasty thoughts from my head, I opened the menu.

"I'm normally still asleep at this time, but *somebody* got me out and about. Since I'm up, I'm hungry."

"I gotchu. What are you in the mood for? Usually, I get the fish and grits breakfast with catfish, but they have a lot of good choices."

"I know I want pancakes or French toast," I told him as I looked over the menu.

It didn't take either of us very long to decide. When the waitress approached our table to take our drink orders, we ordered our food as well. I ended up getting Miss Bertha's breakfast special, which was two hotcakes, two scrambled eggs, bacon, sausage, and grits. Rashaad got his usual.

"The pancakes here are huge. I hope you're hungry," he warned.

"I'm starving, but if I don't eat it all now, I'll take it home and eat it when I wake up from my nap."

"You're serious about Sundays being your lazy day."

"I am because it's my only day off. I try to make the most of it."

"I can understand that. Once we make sure the rink is running smoothly and we can trust the people we hired not to run our shit into the ground, we'll have to make some kind of schedule."

"If you don't, y'all will run yourselves ragged."

"Shit. Just opening the place up had me running on fumes. I think we hired a good crew, though. We vetted their asses like we were the FBI."

"These days, you have to. You never know what people are doing behind the scenes. One of the studios that I worked at in Atlanta got shut down because the owner and a couple of the people he hired were doing some shady stuff behind the scenes. I'm not saying that you're that type of person, but you never can be too careful about who you hire."

"Have you ever thought about owning your own studio?" he asked.

"Honestly, not really."

"Why not?"

"I don't know. It's just not something I've ever given much thought. Teaching dance is my passion, and I truly enjoy focusing on only that and my students. I can tell you right now that I'd hate the business side of running a studio. Dealing with all that paperwork is just not my thing."

"There's nothing wrong with that, baby. I was just asking. Being a business owner is not for everybody. You're doing something you love, and that's all that matters at the end of the day."

I was glad he didn't think I was odd or lacked ambition because I didn't want my own business.

"I also want to have a family one day, and I'm not sure I can balance the demands of owning a studio and the demands of being a wife and mother. I know women do it all the time and are very successful. It's just not something I want to try to juggle."

"I appreciate your transparency. My mother has been a stay-at-home mom since my sister was born, and she has always seemed happy. If you're able to do it, why not?"

Our food came, and after the waitress put everything down and asked if we needed anything else, Rashaad took my hands in his and blessed the food.

"Lord, thank you for allowing me to break bread with this ray of light. I don't know what the future holds, but I pray that this is the beginning of something beautiful. May this meal nourish our bodies and fuel our energy as we press through this day."

I knew I should've had my eyes closed and head bowed, but instead, I was staring at him. So when he opened his eyes and lifted his head, he caught me.

"You're not supposed to be looking at me during the blessing of the food," he informed me with a smirk as if I didn't know that.

"I couldn't help myself; you're so beautiful," I said, mimicking his words to me.

"Oh, you got jokes?"

"Who's joking? I'm serious. You are a beautiful man."

He didn't say anything, but if I didn't know any better, I'd say he blushed a bit under his milk-chocolate skin. We ate in silence for a few minutes, and the food was amazing.

"I wanted to ask you something about Zara," I told him between bites.

"Wassup?"

"I know we've only had one class, but I can already see that she's more advanced than her peers. The fall festival is six weeks from now, and once it's over, I want to move her up to the next level, if that's okay with you."

"Really? That's dope. Of course, it's cool with me."

"She'll be the youngest in the class, but I'm the instructor for that one as well, so I'll keep an eye on her, not that I think there will be any issues."

"That's cool. I'm even more comfortable with it since you're teaching the class."

"Great! But don't mention it to her. I want to wait until after the festival."

"Mums the word. Zara has always enjoyed dancing. As soon as she could balance herself on two feet, she was trying to dance. Her mother and I put her in her first dance class when she was three."

"Wow! She already has three years of experience. No wonder she's better than the other kids."

He laughed. "Naw, I wouldn't call what she's been doing experience. I mean, I can see that she's good, especially in comparison to kids her age. But the classes she took before were more for fun. Just from what I saw the other day, your class is the real deal."

That was the first time he'd mentioned Zara's mother since he told me that she'd left. I can only imagine how that affected Zara, but she seemed to be a very well-adjusted and well-behaved child.

"How is she?" I took a chance and asked. "How is Zara handling her mom being gone?"

He shook his head. "She's gotten used to it, but at first, there was a lot of crying, she had a lot of questions, and I honestly didn't have the answers. It's been a while since she's brought her up, though."

"I'm sorry she's had to experience something like that. With her being so young, I know it's devastating."

"Extremely."

We ate in silence for a few more minutes. Just as Rashaad said, my meal was huge, and although I felt like I'd eaten a lot, it didn't look like I'd even put a dent in it.

"How do you feel about her leaving?" I asked because I couldn't help but wonder how he was affected by it all.

"Normally, whenever someone asks me about Carmen, it pisses me off. Not because I was madly in love with her and she broke my heart, but because she broke our daughter's heart. I don't even want her taking up space in my head."

"That's understandable."

"Remember when I said I haven't always listened to my spirit, and I usually regretted it?" I nodded. "Well, Carmen was one of those times when I should have listened. The best thing that came from that relationship was Zara, and I don't regret my baby girl. But trying to explain this shit to her made me wish I had done some things differently."

He paused and took a swig of water.

"I'm not gon' lie and say that I don't have love for Carmen, because I do. She gave me the most precious gift in the world, but I wasn't *in* love with her, and I knew she wasn't the woman I'd spend the rest of my life with."

"The whole situation is... unfortunate, but from what I can see, from the outside looking in, you're handling it very well. You and your baby girl."

"When Carmen left, Zara and I started family therapy. Since the first few sessions, I only sit in if the therapist thinks it's needed. I think it's helping a lot."

"I'm sure it is. The fact that you, a black man in his mid-thirties, had the forethought and insight to even consider therapy is amazing. More than anything you've shared with me about who you are, that's the most impressive."

He smiled and looked down at his almost-empty plate. After such a heavy conversation, we spent the rest of our time together sharing random things about ourselves. By the time we parted ways, I knew that this was the beginning of something special.

6

RASHAAD

The next couple of weeks were hectic, and I didn't have a chance to connect with Aubrielle face-to-face unless you count FaceTime. I enjoyed our phone conversations because they allowed us to focus on getting to know each other and I was grateful for the advanced technology that the iPhone provided. Still, I was anxious to spend some time with her in person.

My parents stayed in Virginia Beach with my aunt for an extra week, and I had to depend heavily on Rasheeda to help me with Zara. She gladly opted out of attending a few meetings to take Zara to dance class. However, I was determined to take her to the Saturday morning class. I knew I wouldn't be able to spend any time alone with Aubrielle, but I was desperate to lay eyes on her.

"Daddy, did Ms. Aubrielle give you the right number?" Zara asked from the back seat.

"What?" I asked, even though I heard her loud and clear.

"I *saaiidd*, did Ms. Aubrielle give you the right number?"

Why did kids always remember shit that didn't concern them?

"Yeah, Zee, she gave daddy the right number."

"Did you call her?"

Why were kids so nosy?

I looked in the rearview mirror, and Zara was looking right back at me, waiting for my answer.

"Yeah, I called her."

"Were you nice to her?"

"Really, Zee? When is your daddy ever mean?"

She giggled. "You're always nice, Daddy. I hope you were *extra* nice to Ms. Aubrielle. I like her."

"You know what? Daddy likes her, too. You think the three of us should hang out?"

Aubrielle was the first woman I'd had any real interest in being in a relationship with since Carmen and I decided to call it quits.

"Yay! Will I get to see Ms. Aubrielle when I don't have dance class?"

If it were any other woman, having her around Zara this soon would be a definite no. However, she and Aubrielle had an established relationship outside of me. Although we hadn't fully discussed what it was that we were doing, she was already mine, even if she hadn't fully accepted it.

"Maybe. I'll ask her after class, but don't you say anything. Let daddy do it, okay?"

"Okay."

I glanced in the rearview mirror again, and my heart warmed at the big smile on Zara's face. It was good to see her smile because there was a time when I wasn't sure she'd smile again. When Carmen left, she was always sad, unusually quiet, and kept to herself a lot. After months of therapy, she was getting back to her old self.

The rest of the ride was quiet, aside from Zara humming along to some Disney songs that were playing on the radio. When we pulled into the parking lot, I looked at the time and saw that we were thirty minutes early.

"Zee, we're a little early. Do you wanna go inside and see if Ms. Aubrielle is here, or do you wanna wait in the car?"

"Inside, please."

"Inside it is."

When we were standing outside of the studio where her class was held, Zara changed into her dance shoes, and I was sure to remind her not to say anything to Aubrielle about the three of us hanging out.

"Zara, remember what daddy said. *I'll* ask Ms. Aubrielle if she wants to hang out with us, *okay?*"

"Yes, Daddy."

I pulled the door to the studio open, and Zara ran inside while I remained by the door. Aubrielle turned around just in time for Zara to hug her around the waist.

"Hey, sweetheart! What are you doing here so early?"

"Because my daddy wanted to ask you to go on a date with us."

Really, Zee?

All I could do was shake my head as Aubrielle lifted her eyes to find mine before giving Zara her attention.

"Well, I would love to go on a date with *you*," she told her.

"But what about my daddy? He likes you, and I do, too. That's why we should all go together," Zara innocently explained.

"How do you know he likes me?"

Zara looked back at me and shrugged her shoulders before answering, "Because he told me."

Again, I found myself shaking my head. That child couldn't keep a secret if her life depended on it. Aubrielle looked at me as she replied to my daughter.

"Well, I like you, too, sweetheart. Your dad *seems* like a nice man. You think I should like him back?"

Nodding her head with excitement, Zara said, "Yes. My daddy is the nicest man ever."

"Are you sure you're not just saying that because he's your dad?" Aubrielle teased, giving her attention back to Zara.

"No, ma'am. My daddy told me to always be honest, no matter what."

"Okay. Why don't you start getting ready for class, and I'll go talk to him?"

"Yes, ma'am," Zara said as she hurried to the area where they left their belongings during class.

I didn't take my eyes off Aubrielle as she seemed to float toward me. As soon as she was within my reach, I pulled her into a hug and nuzzled her neck with my nose, then planted a kiss there. Initially, she returned my affection by wrapping her arms around my neck, then she abruptly tried to move away.

"Rashaad, we can't be doing this here." She tried to push herself from my arms, but I wasn't having it.

"Why not? Didn't you miss me?" I asked, hugging her again.

"I did, but until we figure out what we're doing, we gotta chill on the PDA. I don't want to confuse Zara."

I loosened my hold on her, but our bodies were still flush against each other. Looking her in her eyes, I said, "The fuck you mean until we figure out what we're doing? Did you miss the memo?"

"Umm, apparently."

I looked in the direction that Zara had gone to make sure she was still occupied before I let Aubrielle know what was up. My left hand went to the nape of her neck, and I pulled her face within an inch of mine while my right hand slid between us, giving her pussy a few strokes.

"That pussy is a little moist, and I know you can feel my dick against your stomach. It seems to me that the only one that's confused is you, baby."

When she opened her mouth to speak, I shoved my tongue inside. Giving no resistance at all, she relaxed into the kiss, releasing a soft moan. That was when I pulled away.

"You've been mine since the moment the beat to "Elevators" dropped and you rushed your pretty ass to the floor. You had me mesmerized by the sway of your hips and the way you moved on your skates with ease. The way you were spittin' those lyrics as if you wrote them was sexy as hell. I knew, right then, that I had to have you. My apologies, Elle, for not making myself clear."

"Was that your way of asking me to be your girl?"

"Naw, that was my way of *telling* you that you already my woman."

Before she could reply, the door hit me in the back, and I released her from my hold. We both moved to the side and allowed a few kids to enter.

"We can discuss this later. I gotta get ready for class."

"Ain't shit to discuss, but okay."

I watched her walk away before leaving the studio and making myself comfortable in the seating area outside. Soon, all the kids had arrived, and she began class. Like the last time I was there, my attention was divided between my daughter and the beautiful stranger, but today, there was nothing strange about her.

7

AUBRIELLE

*A*fter my classes ended for the day, I went home, showered, and took a short nap. When I woke up, it took me a few minutes to find something comfortable but cute for my date with Rashaad and Zara. I ended up settling on a pair of skinny jeans and a plain, fitted white T-shirt. Before leaving my room, I grabbed my skates, although I wasn't sure if I'd be using them this afternoon. In the living room, I found Keyla lounging on the couch with her face glued to her phone. She looked up when she noticed me.

"Where you off to?" she asked.

"Meeting Rashaad and Zara at the rink for a group date."

"Aww, that's cute. How did this come about?"

"I'm not really sure. He got her to class thirty minutes early, and when I asked why they were so early, she said because her daddy wanted to ask me to go on a date with them."

"This man done ate your pussy on his desk and talked to his daughter about you. Girl, we may as well start looking for wedding dresses," she joked.

"It's not that serious."

"Oh, but it is, cousin. I haven't met this man, but the more you tell me about him, the more I believe he's the real deal. Nothing you've told me so far gives me fuck boy vibes. Plus, he's allowing you to be around his daughter outside of class. That's huge."

"Yeah," I replied as I thought about her theory. "You may be right."

"I know I am."

"Have you talked to Rashawn?"

She smiled. "I have, but we've done more texting than talking. Our schedules aren't cooperating right now."

"If he anything like his brother, he'll make it happen if he's really feeling you."

"I guess I'll find out soon enough."

"Do you work tonight?" I asked as I walked toward the front door.

"Unfortunately, I do. Lydia called off, and they asked me to come in, knowing I hate overnight shifts. If I had a man, I would've told their asses no."

"I guess I'll see you in the morning."

When I got to the rink, I sent Rashaad a text to let him know I was headed inside. As I entered the second set of doors, I saw Zara's little body wiggling as she waited next to her father. The moment she saw me, she ditched him and barreled toward me, wrapping her arms around my waist in a hug, just as she did this morning.

"Hey, baby girl. Have you been waiting long?"

She released her hold and looked up at me. "No, ma'am. My Pop-Pop just dropped me off because my daddy was here already."

"Great! Let's go have some fun!"

"Yay!"

Taking my hand, she pulled me in the direction of Rashaad, who'd been watching our interaction, standing in the exact spot that Zara had left him.

"Hey! Can I put my skates in your office?"

He raised his eyebrows while a smirk graced his face, then said, "You sure you wanna go to my office?"

I shivered at the memory of what happened the last time I was there.

"Ms. Aubrielle, are you cold?" Zara asked.

"Huh? Oh, no, sweetheart. I'm fine."

I glared at Rashaad while he laughed at his inquisitive and observant daughter.

"I'll go put them in there and meet you two at the arcade," he offered, taking them off my shoulder.

Zara wasted no time dragging me to our first destination. While she ran from game to game, deciding which she wanted to play first, I kept a close eye on her.

"I can't wait to get your fine ass alone," I heard from behind, followed by a set of strong hands wrapping around me.

"Oh really?" I answered without turning around. I didn't want to lose sight of Zara.

"Hell yeah. After tasting that sweet pussy, waiting this long to feel it around my dick has damn near killed a nigga."

He bit me softly on the neck before softly kissing me.

"You're the one with the busy schedule. Let me know the time and the place, and I'm there," I said, flirtatiously before reaching behind me and squeezing his dick, then walking away.

Zara had found a game that she wanted to play and was standing next to it, waving for us to come over. Rashaad was right behind me, holding up a bag full of tokens.

"Daddy, can you hold me up so I can play this one?" Zara asked.

"Zee, you don't know nothing about Pac Man," he teased.

"I just wanna play."

"Okay, hold on a sec."

He walked away and came back seconds later with a step stool. After he put it on the floor, Zara stood on it while he put in the appropriate amount of tokens in the machine.

"Okay, Zee. You gotta pay close attention. Pac Man is the yellow one with the big mouth. You gotta make sure the ghosts don't get him. You ready?"

Rashaad and I stood on either side of the machine as she nodded her head with excitement.

"Go!" he shouted as he pressed the button.

That was the beginning of a fun but exhausting afternoon. After Zara got tired of being eaten by the ghosts, Rashaad and I played a few games, and he was in his feelings because I scored higher than him. He tried to convince Zara that I cheated, but she wasn't falling for it and told him that I had Black Girl Magic, and that was why I beat him.

We moved on to Skee-Ball after that and had such a good time because we could all play at the same time. Zara thought everything Rashaad and I did was funny and was giggling the whole time. She decided she didn't want to play the arcade basketball game. Instead, she wanted to be my cheerleader.

When her father pretended like his feelings were hurt, she said, "Daddy, us girls have to stick together."

Of course, our fun couldn't end without us doing a little skating. While Rashaad went to his office to get our skates, I helped Zara put on the pair that he checked out for her. I couldn't believe that she didn't have her own pair and planned to say something to Rashaad about it. He returned with his skates on and mine draped across his shoulder.

"I got a bone to pick with you," I told him as he passed me my skates.

"Already? What'd I do?"

"Why doesn't Zara have her own skates?"

"Yeah, Daddy. Why don't I have my own skates?"

He shrugged his shoulders. "She hasn't shown much interest in it. Can you even skate, Zee?"

"Just a little, Daddy, but I want my own skates like you and Ms. Aubrielle," she told him.

"Of course, you do. Let's go see if you can skate first."

As one would expect on a Saturday afternoon, RBL was packed with elementary-age kids and their parents. There were groups of teenagers milling around as well. On the way to the floor, Rashaad grabbed a skater aid for Zara, even though she swore she didn't need one. We slowly made it to the center of the floor, and she released my hand before holding onto the skater aid that her father had put down in front of us.

"Zara, you're a dancer, so you'll probably catch on real quick. You just have to remember to keep your tummy tight because that will help with your balance. If you can keep your balance, you'll be good to go."

"Okay," she said before taking off.

Rashaad and I laughed, both knowing that she'd be skating circles around these other kids soon. We managed to do a little skating while we kept an eye on Zara. She found two other little girls that looked to be her age, and they were having a great time.

"She needs a sibling."

"I agree."

"You agree with what?" I asked.

"I agree that she needs a sibling. You offering your womb?"

"Wait… I said that out loud?"

"You did. And I'm taking you up on your offer."

"I'm sorry… that wasn't meant for you to hear. Please disregard."

I skated away, and Rashaad was right behind me. He didn't have to chase me for long before he was able to grab me by the hand. When he spun me around, I ended up with my back against his chest. We continued to skate in slow motion as he wrapped his arms around my waist and bowed his head to kiss my neck.

"You know, I'm gon' hold you to that."

"Daddy, I'm hungry," we heard from below. Zara's timing was perfect.

"I'm hungry, too. Let's go get some food," I said, maneuvering out of Rashaad's arms.

"Wait!" Zara shouted. "Let me show you what I can do."

She pushed the skater aid to the side, steadied herself, then took a deep breath before pushing off and skating away. When she'd gotten several feet away, she stopped, and Rashaad and I went to her.

"Good job, baby girl. You did pretty well."

"Yes, you did," I agreed.

"Thank you! Daddy, can I come to work with you sometimes and practice?"

"Of course, Zee. Now, let's go eat."

By the time we sat down to eat, we were all starving. Rashaad ordered a large cheese pizza, and when they finally arrived at our table, you would have thought we hadn't eaten in years, even though Zara was full after only two pieces, and I was full after four.

"I guess the rest is mine," Rashaad said, pulling the pizza toward him.

"Daddy," Zara said, who was sitting in the booth with me. "You can't eat all that. You'll be sick."

"I guess you're right, baby girl."

"I finally get to meet your mystery woman."

I looked up to see who the voice belonged to, and looking back at me was a face that could have been Rashaad's twin.

"Uncle Shaawwnn," Zara sang as he approached the table.

"Hey, sweet pea." He blew her a kiss before addressing me. "Hi, I'm Rashawn, Rashaad's younger and better-looking brother."

"Man, if you don't take your behind on somewhere."

Rashaad knocked his hand down before I could shake it.

"I'm Aubrielle. It's nice to finally meet you."

"Thank you for connecting me with Keyla. I'm not sure when we'll hook up, but she's cool to talk to until we can make it happen."

"I'm sure if you put your mind to it, you'll make it happen sooner rather than later."

"That's true. But it was good meeting you. I gotta get back to work since some folks on playdates and shi—stuff," Rashawn joked as he walked away.

"You two could be twins," I said.

"So you checking for my little brother now?"

"What? No. I'm just saying y'all look a lot alike."

"I'm just messing with you. We're fourteen months apart. People used to always think we were twins growing up. I'm the better-looking brother, though."

He looked at me, waiting for me to agree. I let him sweat a little before saying, "Yes, Rashaad, you are."

"I know," he directed to me before addressing Zara. "Are you ready to go to Titi's house? Daddy's gotta do some work soon."

"Aww, Daddy? Why can't I stay with Ms. Aubrielle?"

"Because it's time for you to take a bath and get ready for bed.

When I come get you tomorrow, we can get something to eat before we go home. I'll even let you pick the restaurant."

"Can Ms. Aubrielle come, too?"

He looked at me before he responded with, "She's welcome to come if she wants to, Zee, but we can't take up all of her time. She might be busy."

"Are you busy, Ms. Aubrielle?" she asked with the sweetest look on her face.

"I'm never too busy to hang out with you."

"Yaayy," she cheered.

That seemed to satisfy her, and while we waited for Rashaad's sister, she fell asleep in my arms.

"She really likes you," he commented.

"I really like her, too."

"Do you really like her daddy? We're a package deal, you know."

I pretended as if I had to think about it before saying, "He's cool."

"Just cool, huh. Okay, I guess I can live with that."

Zara adjusted her body, and I looked down at her chocolate face. Her eyebrows looked as if she'd just had them shaped, her lashes were long and full, her nose and lips matched her father's, and she had a head full of hair.

"She looks a lot like you, although I haven't seen her mother."

"I think she's the perfect blend of both of us." He paused. "Thank you for today. Zee had a great time. It's been a while since she's smiled and laughed this much."

"I should be thanking you."

"For what?"

"For allowing me to be in the presence of your daughter outside of dance class. I don't take that lightly, and it says a lot about how you must feel about me."

"Me telling you how I feel wasn't enough?"

"I wouldn't say that it wasn't enough, but this was like the cherry on top."

"You—"

"You could have sent me a text and told me where y'all were," a woman's voice said from somewhere behind me.

Rashaad looked up and shook his head before standing. When the woman reached our booth, he hugged her, then they turned to face me. She was beautiful but didn't look a lot like Rashaad.

"Rasheeda, this is Aubrielle. She's—"

"Zara's dance instructor. We haven't met formally, but I bring Zee to class sometimes, and I was at the open house. Nice to meet you."

"Oh, yeah. I think I remember seeing you there. Thank you. It's nice to meet you, too."

I lifted my hand to shake hers, and she waved it off and squeezed in the booth next to me and Zara.

"I don't do handshakes," she told me as she leaned in for a hug, smashing her niece in the process, causing her to wake up.

"Titi, when you get here?" Zara said, rubbing her eyes.

"I've been here, sweet pea. I was just in my office working. Are you ready to go? I got some popcorn and a movie waiting for us at my place."

"Yay! What movie?"

"It's a surprise, so I can't tell you. My goodness, I need to wash and braid your hair. I'm tired of seeing you in this tired ponytail."

"Tired? I thought it looked good," Rashaad said, pretending to be hurt.

"You try, big bro. That's all that matters."

Rasheeda slid out of the booth, and before Zara did the same, she gave me the tightest hug she could muster up.

"I had fun, Ms. Aubrielle. Thank you for coming on a date with me and my daddy."

Then she kissed my cheek and made me feel all warm and fuzzy inside. I already had a soft spot for her, but her actions just melted my heart.

"Thank you, sweetheart, for letting me hang with you. I had a lot of fun, too."

"We can have fun again tomorrow, okay?" she said, reminding me of the commitment I made.

"Yes, we sure can. I can't wait to see what restaurant you pick."

I could feel her father and aunt's eyes on us as we said our goodbyes. When I looked up, Rasheeda was smiling, then she whispered something in her brother's ear that made him nod his head and smile, as well.

"Well, I'll take this little one and let you two have some time alone. I'm sure I'll be seeing you again, Aubrielle."

"It was nice meeting you."

Once the two of them were on their way, Rashaad slid into the booth next to me and put his arm around my shoulder.

"You gon' hang out with me while I work for a minute, or you heading out?" he asked.

"I can hang for a minute, but if you make me work, you gotta pay me."

He chuckled. "Does it have to be cash? Because I got something better."

"What could be better than cash money?" I rubbed my hands together.

With a sneaky grin on his lips, he took my hand and brushed it across his dick. *Good Lord!* The man wasn't even hard and his shit was resting on his thigh.

"As soon as the opportunity presents itself, I'm gon' show your pretty ass just how much better."

Chills went through my body, and I shivered at the thought of what sex would be like with him. It had been close to seven months since the last time I'd had sex, and although I'd abstained for over a year before, I knew I wouldn't be able to resist this man much longer.

"Looking forward to it," I replied, causing him to raise his eyebrows.

As the rink began to transition from younger patrons to older ones, Rashaad made his presence known throughout the building. He stopped and spoke to several people and shocked the hell out of me when he introduced me as his woman. The first moment we were alone, which happened to be in his office, I asked him about it.

"I'm your woman?"

"Haven't I made that abundantly clear?" he asked as he backed me up against the door and softly pecked my lips.

"I do recall you *telling* me something like that, but I'm not the kind of woman that likes to be bossed around."

"Oh really?"

"Yes, really. You need to *ask* me before it's *official*, official."

"Elle, I know we've only known each other for a minute, but I would feel like the luckiest man in the world if you would be my girl."

"Aww, you even made it rhyme," I cooed.

"Is that a yes?" he asked, with his lip against mine.

Instead of responding with a resounding yes in the traditional way, I wanted to be a little more creative... and freaky. I lowered myself into the squatting position, causing Rashaad to have to take a step back.

"What are you doing?" he asked.

I tugged at the waistband of his joggers, pulling them down, along with his boxer briefs. His dick popped out in a semi-hard state, making my mouth water.

"Elle, baby, what are you doing?"

I was sure he knew exactly what I was doing, so I didn't bother to respond. When I lifted his dick to my mouth, I wasn't surprised by its heaviness. I'd never been up close and personal with one this long and thick. It even had the audacity to curve upward.

"You know what to do with that thing?" he taunted.

Looking up at him, directly in his eyes, I teased the head with my tongue before twirling it around a few times, then taking as much of it as I could in my mouth. What it didn't cover, I covered with my hand.

"Goddamn, Elle," he groaned, putting both of his hands on the door but never taking his eyes off mine.

The more my head bobbed back and forth, the wetter my mouth became, the slicker his dick was in my grasp. I applied just the right amount of suction while twisting my hand at the base.

"Fuucckk!" he grunted.

I felt one of his hands at the back of my head, and he began to control the pace as he fucked my mouth. His excitement was apparent when the head of his dick hit the back of my throat, causing me to gag. I didn't let it slow me down, nor did he. The whole time, our eyes were glued to each other's.

"You must want this nut down your throat, baby," he warned.

I tried to communicate to him with my eyes that, that was exactly what I wanted. As I sucked, my tongue rotated around the head every time my mouth made the trip to the tip. I reached underneath and massaged his balls, causing his dick to throb.

"Suck that shit," he encouraged as the pulsing increased.

I prepared myself for the eruption of his volcano, and just like our last encounter in his office, I was grateful for the loud music. Rashaad clearly wasn't the type of man to hold back his verbal appreciation.

"This shit 'bout to blow, Elle."

And it did. As his seeds filled my mouth, both of his hands gripped my head. I sucked until he pulled himself from my jaws and stumbled to his desk, which was several steps away.

Standing to my feet, I wiped the sides of my mouth with my thumb and index finger and stepped toward him. His manhood was still standing at attention with a small amount of semen oozing from the head.

"You need me to take care of that for you?"

His breathing was labored as he looked down at his dick and shook his head. "Hell, naw. You already got my soul. What more do you want?"

"Your heart."

"If you were my woman, I'd willingly hand it over to you. You ready to do that?" he asked as he got a few pieces of tissue to wipe off his dick.

I watched as he cleaned himself up and adjusted his joggers around his waist. Leaning against him, I wrapped my arms around his neck and planted a gentle kiss on his lips. When I pulled away, I finally answered, "More than ready."

8

RASHAAD

Finally, my night had come to an end. I was tired as hell, and I should have been trying to get home and to sleep. Instead, I was going to Aubrielle's place.

"You seem anxious to leave tonight. You got plans?" Rashawn asked as we walked to the back of the building where our cars were parked.

"Yeah, I'm headed to Aubrielle's."

"I feel you on that. I'm headed to this shorty crib that I met last night."

"Oh, word. Wassup with you and the cousin? What's her name?"

"Keyla. Ain't nothing up with us right now. We're just feeling each other out, talking and texting. Nothing that's gon' stop me from doing me."

Between the two of us, Rashawn was the brother who got around. Don't get me wrong, I'd had my share of women, but sleeping around never excited me. I would only fuck around with one, maybe two women at a time, and that was a strong maybe.

"Aye, bruh. Whatever you do, don't fuck shit up and cause friction between me and my woman," I told him.

"Oh, it's like that already?"

"My spirit is telling me she's something special. I had to lock her down."

"You listening to your spirit this time around, I see. Should've done that shit with your crazy ass baby mama."

"If I had done that, I wouldn't have Zee."

"True. She's definitely the only good thing that came from that relationship."

"I'll see you tomorrow. Next week, we gotta figure out a schedule. All three of us don't need to be here every day."

"I agree. Later."

We connected fists before getting into our cars. Rashawn drove off, and I took out my phone to get Aubrielle's address and shoot her a text to let her know I was on my way.

En route, I stopped at a gas station and bought some condoms. I wasn't sure if we'd have sex, but I sure as hell wanted to be prepared. About twenty-five minutes later, I turned down her street. Thankfully, her car was in the driveway because I could barely see the numbers on the houses. I parked in front of the house and called her before I got out.

"You here?" she asked, sounding groggy.

"Yeah. Come open the door."

Ending the call, I stepped out of my car, popped the trunk, and grabbed my gym bag, where I always kept a change of clothes. Just as I approached her front door, I heard some rustling on the other side, then the locks turning. She pulled the door open and stepped to the side, giving me room to enter.

"Take your shoes off," she commanded, and I did as I was told.

Taking my hand, she pulled me through the dark house and led me to her bedroom, where there was some light coming from the ceiling. I looked up and saw there was a small skylight, and the moon seemed to be position perfectly above it. After locking us inside, she released my hand and left me standing by the door. I could see her silhouette climbing into bed.

"Are you coming to bed?" she said after a minute or so of me not moving.

"You mind if I take a shower first?"

"I don't have a bathroom in my room. It's across the hall. The linen closet is in there, too."

"That's cool. I'll be right back."

After a quick shower, I returned to the bedroom and slid into bed behind Aubrielle. When she felt me behind her, she turned around to face me, then kissed my lips.

"How was the rest of your night?"

"It was good, but we can talk about that in a few hours. Go back to sleep." I kissed her forehead and turned to lay on my back.

"What if I don't want to go back to sleep?" she asked, straddling me.

"Well, if you got something better in mind…"

She grabbed the hem of the oversized T-shirt she was wearing and pulled it over her head. To my surprise, she was naked underneath. I mean, I wasn't expecting her to be wearing a bra, but she didn't have panties on either.

"Damn, Elle. You ready for me?"

She leaned down so that her face was hovering over mine and said, "My pussy has been wet since I left your office." Then she shoved her tongue in my mouth.

While we kissed, she ground her pussy against my growing erection. The only thing between us was a pair of basketball shorts, and I could already feel her juices coming through the mesh material. She pulled her mouth away from mine but didn't sit up, causing her breasts to fall in my face. I gripped each of them and pushed them together, then took turns licking each nipple.

"Mmm," she moaned.

With this being our first time having sex with each other, my ego wanted to take control. So after another minute of tickling her nipples with my tongue, I flipped her onto her back. She let out a little screech but opened her legs wider, allowing me to fit comfortably between them.

Her hands went to my waist, and she began to push my shorts down. Instead of letting her struggle, I assisted her with the task, then tossed them on the floor. Slowly, I eased my body on top of hers. With my dick resting between her slick lower set of lips, I rotated my hips in a circular motion as I looked into her eyes.

She pulled my face to hers, and we devoured each other's mouths. The kiss got sloppier and sloppier with each rotation of our tongues, and her pussy got wetter and wetter. The connection between us was so slick, I began to question whether out not I came.

"I bought some rubbers," I mumbled against her lips when I realized how close I was to sliding inside her slippery walls.

"I'm on the pill."

I lifted my head a little to make sure I heard her right.

"You sure?"

Nodding, she said, "Rashaad, put it in, please."

There was no need for her to beg, but it sounded sexy as hell and made my dick stiffen even more. In one swift move, I pushed inside of her tight, dripping hole.

"Fuck!" I groaned from deep within.

"Damn!" she released at the same time.

Over the past week, every time Aubrielle and I spoke on the phone, we vibed on the highest levels. Our connection was deep, and our spirits aligned in ways I didn't know was possible. However, entering her domain, with nothing between us, had me feeling things I could never begin to explain.

"Elle, this pussy—shit, baby, if I bust quick, don't hold it against me. I'll make up for it later."

I began with the slowest of strokes, scared this feeling would come to an end too soon. Her legs went around my waist, the heels of her feet pressing into my ass, urging me to go deeper. I was obedient, deepening my strokes, trying to focus on anything but how her pussy gripped my dick. Then it happened. As she moaned, with her lips against my ear, I felt her throbbing around the entire ten inches of my dick, and I lost the battle.

"Mmm, shit! My God!"

"Fuck, Elle! I'm 'bout to nut," I warned.

I exploded inside of her, and she gushed around me. I hadn't busted a nut that hard in a long time, and it took a lot out of me. I could have fallen asleep inside of her pussy, right then and there. But I had something to prove, and that was precisely what I did until the sun replaced the moon.

9

AUBRIELLE

I slowly opened my eyes, and directly in front of me was Rashaad, sleeping peacefully, with what looked to be a smile on his face. I stared at him for a while before I turned over and eased out of bed. The ache between my thighs reminded me of the many orgasms I had to earn the bruises that were indeed there.

Grabbing my robe, I stepped out of my room, softly closing the door behind me, and went into the bathroom. After relieving my bladder, I took care of the rest of my hygiene, including a nice, hot shower. By the time I got back to the bedroom, Rashaad was sitting up with his back against the headboard. A smile immediately graced my face when our eyes connected.

"Good morning," I said, walking to the bed and leaning in to kiss his lips.

"It's actually afternoon, but it's good, nonetheless. You showered without me?"

"Oh, I'm sorry. You were asleep. What time is it?"

"Twelve thirty."

"Wow! We slept that long?"

I went to the other side of the bed and picked up my phone off the nightstand, confirming the time.

"I think we earned every hour of sleep we got. Hell, a few more."

I turned to face him and noticed the smug look on his face. The way he worked my body over until the wee hours of the morning, he had every right to feel that way.

"Didn't you tell Zara we were going to breakfast?" I reminded him.

"I don't think I said breakfast, specifically, but she'll be alright."

A quick double knock on the door, just before it swung open, caught our attention.

"Hey, Bri, I—oh shit. My bad. I didn't know you had company. You've never... had... company... before," Keyla stuttered as she back out of the room and closed the door.

Rashaad looked at me and said, "It's good to know your bedroom door ain't a revolving one."

"You know what? Shut up!"

I hit him with a pillow and left the room to see what Keyla wanted. She was in the kitchen looking in the fridge.

"Wassup, Key?"

She closed the fridge and turned to face me before saying, "Don't come in here acting like I didn't just walk in on what I just walked in on. Did you finally let him blow your back out?" she whispered that last part.

"Finally? We haven't been dating that long."

"Did you give the man some pussy or not?

"Cousin, there are no words to describe what went on in that room last night. It was so good that I'm pretending like every other sexual encounter I've ever had didn't happen."

"Well, damn. Let me call his brother back," she joked.

"Did you just get in from your shift?"

"I did, and I'm tired as hell, but I have the next two days off, and I'm about to sleep at least one of them away."

"I don't know how you do it, but I appreciate nurses like you. Did you want something?"

"Not really. I was just coming to see how your date was, but it's pretty obvious it went well."

"We're about to get dressed and pick up Zara from his sister's house. You can formally meet him before we leave."

"I certainly want to meet the man that got you out here all outta character."

"Shut up!"

"I can't wait to hear all about your night!" she added before going to her bedroom.

"It was more like morning, but I got you."

Back in my bedroom, Rashaad was up and standing at the foot of my bed, naked as the day he was born, and *damn* was he a sight for sore eyes. As I closed the door behind me, I closed my eyes and told my pussy to chill out. When I opened them, he was staring at me with that smug ass look again.

"You good, Elle?" he asked, smirking as he took slow strides in my direction. His dick was slapping against his thigh with each step.

I could only nod in response. If I had tried to speak, drool would have seeped out of my mouth.

"You sure about that?"

My back was against the door, and he was standing right in front of me. The robe I was wearing was short, hitting about an inch or two above my midthigh. His hand went underneath it, and his fingers found my treasure, right away. I was sure he wasn't surprised by how wet I was. In fact, he was probably expecting it.

I bit my lip, trying to stifle a moan, as one, maybe two of his fingers slid into my hole, and his thumb massaged my clit.

"Come shower with me."

"I just—"

"It wasn't a question," he informed me.

"Okay."

When his hand appeared from underneath my robe, it went straight to his mouth. The way he licked my juices from his index and middle finger made me jealous. I wanted to replace his fingers with my pussy. He must have read my mind because when we got in the shower, he was on his knees, and his tongue became one with it.

By the time we got to Rasheeda's house, she had fed Zara breakfast and lunch, and neither of them were very pleased with Rashaad. After promising Rasheeda dinner at her favorite restaurant in the near future and promising Zara the same, plus a new leotard for dance class, he was in their good graces again.

When we left Rasheeda's place, I thought we were headed to the rink, but surprisingly, Rashaad decided to take the day off. I had no idea what was on the agenda, so when we turned into the driveway of a big, beautiful house, I became curious.

"Is this your house?" I asked.

"No, Ms. Aubrielle, this my Gigi and Pop-Pop's house."

Before I could respond, Zara had taken off her seat belt, hopped out of the car, and ran to the front door. I turned to look at Rashaad for answers.

"I think maybe it's time for you to meet my parents."

"Rashaad, you play too much."

I knew damn well this man did not bring me to his parents' house, with no warning, after only a couple of weeks of dating.

"I'm serious as hell, baby. Zara was gon' tell them all about you anyway. Baby girl can't hold water."

"Does she even know we're dating?"

"She knows something's going on between us."

"You don't think it's too soon?"

"Listen, Elle. Time means nothing. I follow what's in here." He pointed to his heart. "I know couples that dated for ten years, and as soon as they got married, they were filing for divorce. I also know couples that got married after dating for less than three months, and ten years later, they're as happy as they were the day they met."

"But that's—"

"But nothing. If I can have you around my daughter, meeting my parents doesn't even compare. Let's go."

Without another word, he got out and came around and opened my door. I didn't know why I hesitated, because it wasn't like I had a choice. When I got out, he took my hand and pulled me into a hug.

"I'm following my spirit, and it's never, in all of my thirty-five years, been wrong. If you don't feel the strength of the connection between us—"

"I do. I just wasn't expecting this, that's all."

He kissed my forehead and led me to the front door. As soon as we walked in, Zara ran up to us and dragged me away from her father.

"Gigi and Pop-Pop, this Ms. Aubrielle," she introduced me.

"Hello, Mr. and Mrs. Hanes. It's great to meet you."

Rashaad's parents were gorgeous, and I could see where their children got their good looks from. Based on what he had shared with me, I would guess they were in their mid-fifties, but they didn't look a day over forty. Rashaad and his brother looked more like Mrs. Hanes, and Rasheeda looked just like their father.

"It's nice to meet you too, Aubrielle," Mrs. Hanes said, offering a smile that I couldn't quite read, making me more nervous than I already was.

"Gigi, all of us went on a date, and Daddy promised we could go again, too."

Zara spilled all the business and then disappeared to another part of the house.

"It's nice to meet you, young lady," his father said. "Where have you been hiding this beauty?"

"I haven't been. She's Zee's dance instructor, but we met at the rink on the night of the grand opening."

"Technically," I interjected nervously, "we didn't meet that night, but we did cross paths."

"Oh really? That wasn't too long ago," Mrs. Hanes pointed out, causing my discomfort to increase as she gave her son a questioning look.

"And?"

Mrs. Hanes looked in the direction that Zara had gone before saying, "Don't you think it's a little too soon to have her around Zara? I mean, outside of dance class, of course."

"If I felt that way, she wouldn't be here."

"Aye, boy! Watch your tone with my wife," Mr. Hanes reprimanded.

"My bad, Ma. You know, maybe this wasn't such a good idea," Rashaad said, visibly frustrated. "Zee, let's go," he shouted, loud enough for Zara to come running.

"Hold on, son. Don't go," Mrs. Hanes pleaded.

"Naw, I think we should."

"We're leaving already, Daddy?" Zara asked, confused.

"Yeah. Gigi and Pop-Pop are tired from their trip. We'll give them a few days to rest before we come back to visit."

"Okay. Bye, Gigi." She kissed her grandmother's cheek, followed by her grandfather's. "Bye, Pop-Pop. Daddy says you're getting old, and old people need their rest sometimes."

"Zee, do you have to repeat everything?" Rashaad fussed, taking her hand and pulling her out of the front door.

I was nervous about meeting his parents so soon, but this was unexpected. Rashad was so frustrated that he didn't notice that I lingered a bit. I didn't even know what gave me the courage to speak my peace, but I had to do it.

"It's unfortunate that our first meeting has to end like this. I've only known him for a short time, but I've learned some very important things about Rashaad."

I paused briefly, gathering more courage.

"He mentioned being led by his spirit, and I thought to myself he's just trying to impress me. He was very candid with me about how his and Carmen's relationship began, and it was then that I realized how serious he was about letting his spirit guide him. He ignored his spirit when he met her and now understands the error of his ways. But had he not made that mistake, he wouldn't have his biggest blessing. Zara means more to him than life, and he would never put her in harm's way."

I thought maybe they would have something to say, but they both stood silently, waiting for me to continue.

"He has the utmost respect, admiration, and love for you. To him, you embody Black Love, and he is so proud of the example that you've been for him and his siblings. He's made some mistakes when it comes to love, but he's learned from them. I don't know if I'm Rashaad's forever, but trust that your son is letting his spirit guide him where I'm concerned. It was nice meeting you."

10

RASHAAD

I didn't realize that Aubrielle wasn't behind us when Zara and I walked out of my parents' house. When I noticed, I made sure Zara was securely strapped into her booster seat and went back to the house. I heard Aubrielle's voice just as I was about to open the screen door, which caused me to pause. She spoke with confidence and was in no way disrespectful, but her words further confirmed what I already knew. *Aubrielle was the one.*

I walked in as she said her last words. My father wore a slight smirk on his face. He would never go against my mother in front of anyone, but he had no problem letting her know when she was wrong in private. I had a feeling that once we left, that was what he planned to do. My parents weren't unreasonable people, but my mother sometimes forgot that we were all grown. Even if I was making a mistake by moving so fast with Aubrielle, it was my mistake to make.

"Elle, let's go."

"Wait a minute," my mom said. "Aubrielle, I apologize for my attitude. I don't know you well enough to pass judgment. Everything you said was right, and we've discussed many times how Rashaad let his penis lead him into his previous situation."

"Really, Ma?" I shook my head.

"It's true, son, but you did learn from that situation, and we were blessed with our sweet pea. I trust your discernment, so let's start over. What's a good day for you to come over for dinner?" She directed that last question to Aubrielle.

I wasn't surprised at all by my mother's quick change of heart. She'd never had a problem admitting when she was wrong, and I loved that about her.

"The only day I have off is Sunday."

"Okay, next Sunday it is."

Aubrielle looked at me for confirmation, but it wasn't my choice. If she didn't feel comfortable, I would understand. I shrugged my shoulders, letting her know that it was up to her.

"I guess I'll see you both next Sunday," she finally said.

The hug from my mother that followed her confirmation surprised everyone. My father still hadn't said anything, but as my mother and Aubrielle embraced, he gave me the thumbs-up sign.

We finally said our goodbyes and headed to the car. Zara was sound asleep with her headphones on, her head cocked to the side, and her mouth wide open. I was glad she was sleeping and I could talk to Aubrielle without her little nosy ass eavesdropping, although it may be rough putting her to bed tonight.

"That was interesting," Aubrielle spoke before I had a chance.

"It wasn't what I was expecting. That's for sure."

"I can't even be mad at your mom, though. She's just looking out for her son and her granddaughter. Nothing wrong with that."

I glanced at her quickly to see if she was serious. When I didn't see her cracking a smile, I figured she was.

"You're right. Nothing is wrong with her looking out for us, but she's too old to act the way she acted today. Had I not decided to leave, she was about to show her ass. I love her with everything in me, but she was wrong."

She shrugged her shoulders before saying, "No reason to dwell on it. Everything's cool now, and I'm getting a free meal out of it."

"It's cool because you let her know what's up," I said, glancing at her again.

"You heard me?"

"Every word. And that shit was sexy as hell. You're lucky I'm on daddy duty tonight, or I'd take you back to my place and fuck the shit outta you."

She rolled her eyes and shook her head. "Where *are* you taking me exactly?"

"I gotta get Zara ready for the week, but I figured we could grab a quick bite to eat before I take you home."

"Sounds good. I'm exhausted, and I still have to do some laundry and catch up on all my shows."

"Damn, I thought you'd at least be a little disappointed that we had to part ways," I said, pretending to be hurt.

"I am, but my pussy needs a break, and I know if the opportunity presents itself, you'll be burying yourself between my legs."

"You damn right, I would."

We ended up stopping at Shake Shack for dinner. When Zara opened her eyes and saw where we were and that Aubrielle was still with us, her face lit up with excitement. Just like the day before, the three of us had a good time. Later that evening, when we arrived at Aubrielle's house, we all went inside because Zara convinced Aubrielle that she *needed* to see where she lived.

"Daddy, when can Aubrielle come to our house?" Zara asked as she looked around.

Does every six-year-old ask too many questions?

"I don't know, Zee. Maybe we can cook dinner for her this week and invite her over."

"Yay! Aubrielle, me and Daddy are gonna cook for you," she said as if Aubrielle hadn't heard me.

"That'll be nice. I hope you two can cook."

"I'll make sure he doesn't burn it, okay," Zara assured.

"Wow, Zee. You just putting me on blast like that."

After a quick tour and a million more questions, Zee was satisfied, and we prepared to leave. At the door, I kissed Aubrielle on her forehead, even though I wanted to do much more, and promised to call her once I had Miss Busybody down for the night. Overall, it ended up being a good day.

11

AUBRIELLE

When I arrived at Groove Motion for my first class a few days later, a pipe had burst somewhere on the second floor, so we had to cancel classes for the day. It wasn't even one o'clock, and it felt strange to have a full day to myself during the middle of the week. I decided to stop by RBL to see what Rashaad was up to.

Although the rink wouldn't be open for a few more hours, the doors were unlocked, and I walked right in. What I saw when the floor came into view shocked the hell out of me. For several minutes, I stood in awe, watching Rashaad. "Nice & Slow" by Usher blasted from the speakers, and what I was observing was turning me on with each passing second.

I could tell that he was lost in the moment. I'd been around male dancers for my entire life, and I'd never seen a man move with more grace than what I saw from Rashaad, and he was wearing skates. If I had to guess, I'd say that he was professionally trained, although he'd never mentioned it.

One move after another, he was so damn smooth with it. But when he did the two-foot spin for so long that I damn near got dizzy, then transitioned on to one foot and still had enough momentum going to spin for another minute, I was ready to take my panties off and throw them at him. I'd never seen a pirouette so beautiful. You couldn't tell me that he hadn't taken ballet at some point in his life.

As Usher's song faded out, I thought Rashaad might look my way, but he was still in his own world and hadn't noticed that I'd come in. "Some Cut" by Lil Scrappy and Trillville started to play, and all the elegance and gracefulness he'd just displayed went right out the window. The moves he did to that song reminded me of the fraternities on the campus of my alma mater, except he was on skates. Talk about sexy. I had to fan myself because I was getting hot and fucking bothered.

It wasn't until I decided to put on my skates and join him that he realized I was present. As I glided onto the floor, he blessed me with his beautiful smile, making me feel warm all over.

"What are you doing here?" he asked.

He continued to glide backward, and when I was close enough, he took both of my hands and pulled me along, leaning in for a quick kiss.

"A pipe burst at Groove Motion on the second floor. We had to cancel today's classes."

"Zee ain't gon' like that."

"Oh, I hadn't even thought of that. Is it crowded here on Wednesdays? I can probably take her to one of the corners and go through part of the routine."

As we conversed, the song changed, and Tamar Braxton's sultry voice came through the speakers. As "The One" began to play, Rashaad swung me to his left, placing me on the inside of his body, and we shadow skated. I mirrored his moves, and it was unreal how in sync we were.

"Naw, baby. You don't have to do that. Enjoy your day off. I already talked to Shawn and Sheeda about covering for me here tonight, so Zara and I can make dinner for you."

"Oh, yeah, that is tonight. Zara probably won't care about dance class. But I got a bone to pick with you, though."

"Damn, another one? What'd I do this time?"

"Have you ever taken a dance class? Ballet maybe?"

He tried to hide his smirk, but it came through and turned into a broad smile.

"How long you been here?" he asked instead of answering my question.

"No, you can't answer a question with a question. Answer me."

"It's a little-known fact that I took ballet."

He stopped skating and leaned against the wall. When I stopped in front of him, I put my arms around his neck, and he secured his around my waist.

"I knew it! Why didn't you tell me?"

"It ain't come up."

"I can think of a few conversations we've had when you could have *segued* right into that, but it's cool if you didn't want me to know."

"Naw, it wasn't that. I just don't think about it much. When I was about six or seven, these older kids in the neighborhood started fucking with me and Shawn. We never told anyone, but one day, I was fed up with the shit, and I beat one of their asses. A few more came for me, and I beat their asses, too. Somehow, it got back to my parents that I was terrorizing the kids in our neighborhood."

"Why didn't you tell your parents what was going on?"

"'Cause I wasn't no snitch, and I was handling it. My mom had the bright idea to put me in a ballet class to channel some of my energy and anger."

"That's odd. Why ballet and not football or basketball?"

He shrugged his shoulders. "I ain't sure. I think she wanted me to hate it, but my ass ended up liking it and mastering that shit. I stopped being a badass, too, but mainly because word got out that I was beating everybody's ass, and people stopped messing with us."

"Wow. That's so... different. When did you stop taking lessons?"

"When I was about twelve or thirteen. It was before I started high school. I wouldn't say I lost interest, but it had served its purpose. That was around the time I fell in love with the art of roller skating. There was a rink we used to go to all the time, and I was able to combine the two art forms."

"You know, every time we're together, I become more and more impressed. You're an interesting man, Rashaad Hanes."

"You think so?"

"I do."

His hands moved down to my ass, and he gave it a squeeze.

"Am I interesting enough for you to let me take you to my office, bend you over my desk, and let me hit it from the back?"

I laughed but was turned on by his question. Looking around, I saw some of his employees getting ready to start their workday. It was probably safe for us to have a quickie.

"Where's Rashawn and Rasheeda?"

"Shawn's here somewhere. Sheeda's not coming until we open."

Although I hadn't agreed, Rashaad pushed away from the wall, causing me to roll backward. I heard "Are U Still Down?" by Jon B. and Tupac in the background. Then Rashaad had the nerve to start singing. He didn't sound nearly as good as Jon B. as he sang, "I can see that you want me, by the way that you smile," but he had me grinning from ear to ear.

Thankfully, he gave up on the serenade, allowing me to appreciate the singer's sexy voice instead. He positioned himself behind me, pulling me tightly against his chest. As we glided backward to the beat of the music, swaying from side to side, I felt his arm around my waist, and his hand ultimately found a resting spot right on top of my mound. I rested my head on his shoulder, then reached up and caressed the back of his neck.

I could feel his stiffening dick against my back. When his lips made contact with my neck at the same time that his hand began a slow massage of my pussy, I release a moan.

"You know you want this dick," he whispered against my ear.

We continued our slow, sexy skate around the perimeter of the floor, and as soon as we made it to an opening, we veered off and made a beeline to his office. Rashaad didn't even bother getting out of his skates or clothing because he was focused on getting me out of mine. He kneeled in front of me, undid the laces of my skates, nudging me to step out of them while I pulled my hoodie over my head and tossed it to the side. Once my arms were out of my leotard, I pushed it down my body, taking my leggings and thong with it.

Rashaad remained on his knees, with his face only a nose length away from my pussy. Completely naked, I stood before him, waiting for him to put out the fire between my legs. Preparing myself for the tongue lashing that I knew I was about to get, I took a deep breath and closed my eyes. When I heard some movement after a few long seconds, I opened them to find him seated, with his pants only down low enough for his dick to make an appearance.

"Ride this shit!" he demanded.

And I did.

12

RASHAAD

Aubrielle popping up at the rink was a welcomed surprise, and the way she put that pussy on me was an added bonus. After our afternoon rendezvous, she went home to get cleaned up, while I picked up Zara from school and went to the grocery store.

"Daddy, what are we making for Ms. Aubrielle?" Zara asked as we unpacked the groceries.

"I thought we could make an avocado salad with chicken fajitas and chips and salsa as an appetizer."

"Yes!" she cheered with excitement.

Unlike most six-year-olds, Zara ate just about anything, and she loved vegetables. Her mother and I had fairly healthy diets, and she never had a problem eating whatever we ate.

"You think Ms. Aubrielle will like it?"

"Ummhmm," she said with a nod.

After we finished putting away the groceries, I helped Zara with her homework, then we prepared dinner. My life had been so busy that it had been a while since the last time Zara and I had cooked together. Now that we had a schedule worked out at RBL, I needed to be more intentional about spending quality time with my baby girl.

"Daddy, do you miss Mommy?"

It had been a few months since Zara had mentioned anything about her mother. When Carmen first left, every day, Zara asked about her. After about a month, she'd bring her up every few days. At some point, it was once a week, and before long, she stopped asking about her at all. I didn't know how to answer Zara's question truthfully without sounding like I didn't care that her mother was gone.

"I wish your mother was here so you could see her every day. I know her being gone makes you sad, and I want you to always be happy."

"I'm not that sad anymore, but sometimes I forget what it was like when she was home. I'm a little bit mad at her."

That was new. She went to therapy twice a week for four months, now she only went twice a month, and she'd never mentioned being angry in any of the sessions I was in, nor had her therapist said anything about it.

"Why are you mad at your mother, baby girl?"

She shrugged her shoulders as she thought about what to say. "Because now I don't have a mom, and all of my friends at school do."

I stopped what I was doing and went to her. Picking her up, I sat her on top of the counter so that we could somewhat be eye level. She said she wasn't sad, but there were tears in her eyes.

"I'm sorry, Zee. Your mother may not be around, but you have me, Gigi and Pop-Pop, plus your uncle and titi. I know it's not the same as having your mother, but we love you so much, baby girl."

"What if I told my friends at school that Mommy was dead? Because it feels like she died, Daddy," she cried.

Damn!

"You know you don't have to have to tell your friends anything, because it's none of their business, but you tell them whatever makes you feel comfortable. Okay?"

She nodded and wrapped her little arms around my neck. My heart hurt for her, and I hated that Carmen was the reason for the way Zara was feeling. When she released my neck, she looked up at me with sad eyes.

"What about Ms. Aubrielle?"

"What about her?"

"You said I have Gigi, Pop-Pop, Uncle, and Titi, but you didn't say Ms. Aubrielle."

Even though my spirit was shouting at the top of its lungs that Aubrielle was my forever, I had no idea how to explain that to a six-year-old.

"Listen, Zee, what I'm about to say to you, you may not understand, but as your father, I want to always be honest with you."

I paused and waited for her to indicate that she was listening. When she nodded, I continued.

"I like Ms. Aubrielle, and I think she likes me, too. Even though we haven't known each other for a very long time, my heart says she is someone very special."

"My heart says she's special, too, Daddy."

"Oh really?"

She nodded, and I wrapped my arms around her so tight she probably couldn't breathe, then lifted her from the counter.

"Let's get this food ready before our special lady gets here."

WHEN AUBRIELLE ARRIVED, I let Zara open the door for her while I stood off to the side. This was the first time she'd been to our home, and Zara was ready to give her a tour.

"Hi, Ms. Aubrielle. Welcome to our home," she greeted her.

"Hey, sweetheart. Don't you look adorable?"

Aubrielle bent down a little to hug Zara. When they separated, Zara did a few poses in the dress that she convinced me she had to wear.

"Why didn't you tell me we were dressing up?" Aubrielle asked Zara.

"Just I did. I wanted you to see me all pretty."

"Zara, you're beautiful every time I see you. It doesn't matter what you're wearing. Okay?"

"Thank you. You want a tour?"

"Of course. Let me say hello to your dad first, though."

"Okay. I'll be right back."

Zara skipped away toward her bedroom.

"Hey, handsome."

"Wassup, beautiful? How was the rest of your afternoon?"

She stepped into my arms for a hug, and I kissed her forehead before releasing her.

"It was fine. After I showered, I took a nap. Thank God Keyla came home, or I'd probably still be asleep."

I laughed. "You wore yourself out trying to wear me out. Serves your little ass right."

"Whatever! I'm not worn out. I just didn't know what to do with myself, because I'm not normally home at that time."

"Believe what you want, baby." I chuckled at her denial.

"Ms. Aubrielle, I changed so I could be comfortable," Zara said when she reappeared in a pair of sweats and a long-sleeved T-shirt.

"And you still look adorable. Now, what did you two make for dinner? It smells amazing in here."

"It's a surprise. First, we have to do a tour," she said, taking her by the hand and guiding her away from the front door.

"Hang on," Aubrielle said as she slipped out of her shoes. "Okay, I'm ready."

I followed them as Zara took her to each room of our open-layout house. It had four bedrooms, one of which I'd made into an office, three and a half bathrooms, a family room or den, a dining room, an eat-in kitchen, and a nice-sized basement.

"Everything looks so new. How long have you lived here?"

"About four months. We'd been living downtown since Zara was born, but it was time for a change."

The only reason we stayed downtown for so long was because Carmen was an aspiring model and actress and wanted quick access for early morning shoots. Initially, I didn't have a preference, but as Zara got older, I didn't want to be so close to the city's hustle and bustle, and I wanted her to have a yard to play in. Although Carmen and I often argued about it, I started looking a couple of months before she decided to leave. She was welcome to come with us if she wanted to, but Zara and I were moving, with or without her.

"This is really nice. You made a good choice, and you have great taste."

"Thank you. I can't lie, though. Sheeda helped me with Zara's room and the guest room. Everything else is all me."

"I like it. It's manly but has some softness about it, just like your personality," she said as we ended the tour and headed to the kitchen.

I was walking behind her and pulled the back of her shirt, stopping her from moving. Wrapping my arms around her waist from behind and kissing her neck, I asked, "You trying to call me soft?"

Moving away from me and catching up with Zara, she replied, "Not at all. You're as hard as nails, but you do have a sensitive side. I like it, so no worries."

In the kitchen, Zara stood on the stool that we kept near the sink to wash her hands, and Aubrielle and I followed her lead.

"My stomach is growling, Zara. Can you tell me what we're having now?"

"Me and my daddy made chicken fajitas with avocado salad. You can go sit at the table, and I'll get the chips and salsa."

"My goodness. I can't wait to dig in."

Aubrielle sat at the kitchen table and waited for Zara and I to bring out the food. Zara couldn't carry them at the same time, so she took the bowl of chips to the table first, then went back for the salsa while I took the salad.

"Ms. Aubrielle, Daddy says this is the ap—the appe—Daddy, what is it called again?"

"The appetizer, Zee."

"Yeah, that. You can eat some of that while we get the real food."

She started to walk away but then remembered something and turned back to Aubrielle.

"And you can't eat a lot of it because you'll be too full." Then she got to me and said, "Come on, Daddy. We have to hurry so she won't get full off the chips."

"I'm ready, baby girl. Daddy has to carry this stuff because it's hot. You take these and put them on the table."

I handed her two trivets and followed her to the table. Once she placed them down, I put the hot pan with the cooked vegetables on one of them and the skillet where I kept the tortillas warm on the other.

"Zee, you have a seat, and I'll get the rest."

She did as she was told, and I went and got the tray with all the extra trimmings: shredded cheese, sour cream, guacamole, and pico de gallo. After placing it on the table, I sat across from Zara.

"Y'all ready to eat?" They both nodded. "Let's blessed the food."

After I said a short prayer over the food, Aubrielle asked, "Zara, did you help your dad make all of this?"

"Ummhmm," she said proudly. "I'm his helper."

"You did a great job. Everything looks delicious."

Aubrielle uncovered the tortillas, grabbing three of them and putting them on each of our plates. She then took the lid off the vegetables and reached for the tongs.

"Elle, you're our guest. What are you doing?"

"I'm helping Zara make her fajita. I don't mind."

She continued, asking Zee what all she wanted on her fajita. When she finished, her plate looked picture perfect.

"Thank you," Zara said before she ate a fork full of avocado salad.

When Aubrielle reached for my plate, I moved it, saying, "Thank you for helping Zee, but I can make my own. As I said, you're our guest."

She rolled her eyes and said, "Suit yourself," then proceeded to hook up her fajita. The way she had everything positioned just right almost made me change my mind. Once she added the salad to her plate, it looked like it was served at a Mexican restaurant.

"Did you used to work at Chili's or shi—or something?"

She laughed and said, "Not Chili's, but this other Mexican restaurant in Atlanta. I wasn't a cook, but we had to know how to stage all the entrees."

She began to eat as I prepared my plate. It must have tasted good because she moaned, causing me to pause and give her a look. Her eyes met mine, but she quickly looked away.

"Do you like it, Ms. Aubrielle?" Zara asked.

I wanted to say, *hell yeah, she liked it. Didn't you hear her moan?*

"These are the best fajitas I've ever had. I can't believe you two made this."

"Fajitas are my favorite," Zara said.

"Really? Most kids your age wouldn't even try fajitas because of the vegetables."

"But they're so yummy. Vegetables are my favorite."

"That's good, Zara. You'll stay healthy and strong because you eat all your vegetables."

Zara nodded while taking another fork full of salad. We continued eating with light conversation. When we finished, Aubrielle insisted on helping us clean the kitchen. By the time that was completed, it was time for Zara to get ready for bed. She'd taken a bath before dinner, so all she needed to do was brush her teeth and put on her pajamas. After she'd done both, she came skipping back into the kitchen.

"Daddy, can I read my story to you and Ms. Aubrielle?"

"Yes, baby girl. Go pick out a book and get in bed. We'll be in there in a few minutes."

"Okay!" she said with excitement.

I leaned against the counter and reached for Aubrielle. She willingly stood between my legs and rested her body against mine, putting her arms around my neck.

"You're such an amazing father. It's a beautiful thing to see."

"Thank you. I do my best."

"Dinner was great, and my company was even better."

"Well, we'll have to do it again."

"I'll see when Keyla works nights again, and I'll cook for you and Zara."

"What are you gonna make? Peanut butter and jelly sandwiches?" I joked.

"Ha-ha! You're not funny but maybe I will."

"Naw. I'm just playing, baby. That sounds like a plan. Let's go let her read to us before she comes back in here."

She followed me to Zara's room, and we found her fast asleep with the book she'd chosen on her chest.

"I knew she was tired. The excitement of you visiting wore her down."

I slowly slid the book out of her arms and walked it over to her bookcase.

"How could her mother just leave her like that?" Aubrielle asked as she looked down at Zara sleeping peacefully.

The tone of her voice let me know that her question was rhetorical. She was right behind me as I walked out of Zara's room. We went to the family room, and I sat in the recliner, then pulled her onto my lap.

"I'm sorry. I didn't—"

"It's cool. No need to apologize. Every time I look at Zara, I think the same thing."

"I can't imagine what Zara's little mind is thinking."

"She mentioned her today, and she hasn't done that in months."

"Really? What did she say? I mean, if you don't mind me asking."

"Naw, I don't mind at all. Any questions you ever have about me and Carmen, feel free to ask. Zee asked me if I miss her."

"Do you?"

I shook my head. "I miss that my daughter doesn't get to see her mother every day like most kids her age, but that's it."

"But you guys were together for a long time. You must miss her a little," she tried to reason.

"We lived together for a long time, but Carmen and I stopped trying to be in a relationship when Zee was about a year old. The day she left, she told me that she'd resented me from the day that I convinced her not to have an abortion."

Aubrielle gasped and covered her mouth with her hand.

"She'd never said anything like that before and that shit hurt. It was important to me for Zee to have both of us in the same house, so once we stopped trying to force a relationship, Carmen moved into the third bedroom of our condo. We managed to get along and co-parent well, for the most part."

"Were she and Zara close? Did they do mother-daughter things?"

"Zara is the true definition of a daddy's girl. I used to think that it bothered Carmen that she was so attached to me, but now, I don't think she cared. She did the minimum when it came to trying to bond with her."

"That's so sad."

"Don't get me wrong. Carmen didn't mistreat Zara. I would've never let that happen. But when I think back, there was never a real connection. I thought it would change as Zara got older, but... here we are."

"Did you ever meet her parents? Maybe her relationship with them has something to do with it."

"She told me she was a ward of the state from the time she was twelve, I think, until she turned eighteen. Before that, I think she lived with some relatives. It's sad to say that I don't know much more about her. Whenever I would ask, she'd change the subject, and eventually, I stopped asking."

"Wow. I'm no psychiatrist, but her upbringing says a lot. Maybe that's why she was so detached. Although, I would think it would make her more attached to a child of her own."

I nodded in agreement, but I was tired of talking about Carmen.

"You staying the night with me?"

"Umm..."

"Umm what? Zara knows wassup."

"That's because she's a very perceptive little girl. I think it's too soon for all that, but whenever you have a sitter for her, I'll be happy to stay."

"Are you serious?"

"Are you pouting?"

She kissed my lips before I could reply, and it turned into a full make-out session. My hands went under her shirt, then her bra. Her hands squeezed between us, and she rubbed my dick through my sweats.

"Stay the night," I whispered against her lips.

"Uh-uh," she moaned.

"You staying."

"Uh-uh," she moaned again, shaking her head.

I pulled away from her and gave her the saddest eyes I could give. Instead of giving in, she tried to get up from my lap, but I held her down.

"Where you going?"

"I told you I wasn't staying. I don't want to be creeping outta here in the wee hours of the morning, and I don't want Zara to wake up and find me here."

This time when she tried to stand, I let her. I knew she was right, but my dick didn't want to accept it. After fixing her clothes, she headed for the front door. Begrudgingly, I got up and adjusted my dick as I went to see her out. Once she got her shoes on, I stepped into her personal space.

"You're right."

"I know I'm right, but if I had agreed to stay—"

"We would've been wrong together, and I'd be digging in them guts instead of walking you to your car."

"Why you gotta say shit like that?" She shook her head.

"Making you have second thoughts?" I teased and kissed her nose.

Ignoring me, she pulled the door open and walked out.

"Don't get mad at me because you leaving with your pussy throbbing," I continued as I followed her out.

"Boy, ain't nobody's pussy throbbing."

I lifted her off the ground, pinned her against the driver's side door, put my hand between us, and then cupped her pussy. Our faces were just inches apart.

"She's not throbbing?"

She shook her head.

"I don't believe you."

I moved my hand to the waistband of her leggings and pulled them and her panties down enough from me to slide my hand between her legs, brushing my fingers against her outer lips.

"She might not be throbbing, but she wet as fuck."

Our lips connected, and my tongue immediately went looking for hers. As they did a sexy dance, my index and middle fingers slithered inside of her drenched hole while my thumb pressed on her clit. She moaned into my mouth as I dipped my digits in and out and my thumb moved in a circular motion over her ripe bud.

"Mmm, shit!"

Her head flew back, landing on the hood of the car as she rode my fingers to ecstasy. The reward from my efforts dripped down my fingers, onto my hand. She had to grab my wrist and beg me to stop because I was trying to pull another orgasm out of her.

Slowly, I removed my hand, then wasted no time putting my fingers in my mouth. I might have to bust a nut in the shower tonight, but at least I got to taste Aubrielle's sweet nectar before doing so.

13

AUBRIELLE

*D*inner at the Hanes' residence was going well, so far. We'd been there for about an hour, and Zara had been doing most of the talking. Rashaad was right about her not being able to hold water. She told her grandparents all about the night I had dinner at their house, from what they cooked for me, to everything we talked about, to her falling asleep before she could read us a story. Eventually, Rashaad took her outside to play, leaving me alone with his parents.

Mrs. Hanes seemed to be warming up to me. Although I hadn't said much, the vibe between us was a lot more relaxed than our first meeting. I noticed that she watched my interactions with Zara very closely. I couldn't even be mad about that because I understood. Zara had been through enough already, and Mrs. Hanes wanted to protect her. Mr. Hanes was as cool as the other side of the pillow.

"How did your parents feel about their only child moving away?" Mrs. Hanes asked.

"Surprisingly, they were okay with it. My father thought it was past time for me to spread my wings a little since I didn't go away for college."

"What made you choose D.C.?" she asked.

"My cousin, Keyla, went to Howard and never moved back home. I've visited her often over the years, and I found something new to love about it every time."

"There's so much to love here. I don't blame you. Atlanta has a lot to offer as well," Mr. Hanes added.

"It does. I love my city. When I was deciding what college I wanted to attend, it didn't even cross my mind to look outside of Atlanta. Emory University had everything I wanted in a college. It being in my hometown was a bonus."

"How often do you get back to Atlanta?" he asked.

"Every few months. I'm actually due for a visit in a couple of weeks. My parents are throwing a big party for their thirty-fifth wedding anniversary."

"Oh, wow! We just celebrated our thirty-sixth a few months ago. Congratulations to them. Staying married this long in this day and age is no easy feat," said Mrs. Hanes.

"Especially when your wife is as crazy as mine," Mr. Hanes added.

We all laughed at his joke and continued to converse a bit longer. Once Mrs. Hanes announced that dinner was ready, Zara and Rashaad came in, smelling like outside. Once they washed up, we met in the dining room and enjoyed a salad, fried catfish, spaghetti, homemade hush puppies, and corn on the cob. For dessert, she made a caramel cake. It wasn't extravagant, but damn, it was good. I'd be spending some extra time in the studio to work off this meal.

Because Rashaad had to go back to RBL, Zara was staying overnight at his parents' house. He went through her nightly routine with her while I helped Mrs. Hanes clean the kitchen. As we were finishing up, Zara came to get me to read Rashaad and me a story. After confirming that he'd be there to take her to school in the morning, he kissed her forehead, and we wished her a good night.

"I enjoyed your company tonight, Aubrielle, and I apologize again for last week," Mrs. Hanes offered as Rashaad and I prepared to leave.

"Last week is forgotten and forgiven. I had a great time, and the food was delicious."

"Maybe when you come back from visiting your parents, we can do this again."

"I'd like that."

We said our goodbyes with hugs and cheek kisses, then Rashaad and I were on our way. I was a bit surprised at how well the evening went, but I was happy about it.

"That was nice," I said when once we were both in the car.

"I enjoyed it. Our schedules are always busy, so my mom doesn't cook like that too often. I think she misses it."

"Aww, you guys should make time to spend time with them."

"We do, but our schedules never match up, especially now that the rink is open. It's usually one or two of us, but never all three of us."

"You guys should make time, at least once a month, to spend some time with them," I suggested. "I bet they'd love it."

"Yeah, I'm sure they would. I'll have to talk to Shawn and Sheeda." He paused, then glanced over at me. "When are you going to visit your parents?"

He was outside playing with Zara when it came up earlier, and I hadn't mentioned it to him before.

"Weekend after next."

"You already booked your flight?"

"No. Keyla and I planned to book them tomorrow morning. It's their thirty-fifth wedding anniversary, and they're throwing themselves a big party."

"You weren't gon' invite your man?" he asked, sounding a little hurt.

"Rashaad, you're a very busy man. You have a daughter that you're raising alone, and you just opened up the hottest skating rink in D.C. I didn't think you'd be able to squeeze my parents' anniversary party, *in Atlanta*, into your schedule."

"Baby, I can make time to meet my future in-laws."

I laughed out loud. "You play entirely too much."

"Shit, who playing?"

I looked his way, and he was focused on the road. The fact that this man was so sure that he and I had a future together gave me all the feels. I'd never been in a relationship that progressed so quickly, and what was even more shocking to me was that my feelings were on the same fast track. When we pulled up to a stoplight, he turned to look at me with his lips curled into a sexy smirk.

"It's in my spirit, baby," he said with confidence. "And this time, there's no denying it."

14

RASHAAD

Somehow, my brother finessed his way into joining us on the trip to Atlanta. Rashawn and Keyla had been out a couple of times, but apparently, she'd been sending him off the last few times he tried to hook up with her. I asked him what he did to scare the woman off, and he swore he was the perfect gentlemen. For some reason, I didn't believe him. When I told him I needed to take some days off to go to Atlanta and why, his interest was piqued.

The next thing I knew, Rashawn and I were standing in Rasheeda's office, trying to convince her that she could handle the rink for a weekend alone. It took a minute, but she eventually agreed, although we had to make a bunch of promises that she would be cashing in on in the future. We also made sure Barry, our head of security, and his team would be there in full force, and our father agreed to help out as well.

Now that the time had come, I was a little nervous about leaving my little sister in charge on our busiest days, but Rasheeda was smart and knew what she was doing. No matter how old, she would always be my baby sister, and sometimes, I had a hard time remembering that she was a grown and educated businesswoman. She told us she'd call us if she needed something, but if we called her, she would ignore it. Thankfully, my father and Barry agreed to keep me posted.

"I still can't believe you forced your way onto this trip."

We were on our way to pick up Aubrielle and Keyla, then head to the airport.

"Force? I ain't force shit. I just booked a flight and a hotel room."

I laughed. "Nigga, you weren't invited. What did Keyla say when you told her?"

"I didn't tell her. Aubrielle told her, and she called questioning me."

"Damn, bruh! Do you blame the woman? Y'all ain't even dating, and here you are intruding on her trip. She might have planned to hook up with an old flame or some shit."

"Shaad, we going to ATL, bruh. It's like the pussy headquarters of America."

The pussy headquarters of America? The fuck?

"Bruh, I've heard a lot of things about Atlanta, but that ain't one of them."

"It don't matter. If Keyla on some bullshit, I ain't never had no problem finding pussy."

"Shit, in Atlanta, you better make sure it's pussy attached to the woman and not dick. I done heard some things."

"Damn, bruh." He shook his head with a frown. "You just fucked me up with that visual."

"Just telling you what I heard," I warned.

Rashawn and I were truly polar opposites. I loved women just as much as the next man, but I'd never been out there the way Rashawn was. He'd probably be in his forties before he considered settling down.

A short time later, I parked in the driveway of Aubrielle and Keyla's house. Aubrielle opened the door as we approached, and when our eyes met, her face lit up with a big smile. When I stepped inside, I backed her against the wall and kissed her like I hadn't seen her in months, though it had only been a few hours.

"Get a room!" Rashawn said.

When we separated, she reached up and swiped her thumb across my lips to remove her lip gloss.

"Good morning, baby," she greeted.

"Good morning, to you. Y'all ready?"

"Yeah. Our suitcases are by the door. I just need to switch purses real quick."

"Cool. I'm about to use the bathroom while you do that."

A few minutes later, I found her in her closet, reaching for something off the top shelf.

"You need help?"

She jumped when she heard my voice. "Shit, you scared me. Yeah, can you grab that purse in the corner for me?"

"I got it, shorty."

"Whatever."

She took the purse from me and went to her bed, quickly taking things from one purse and putting them in the one I'd just given her.

"We got time, baby. You don't have to rush," I told her.

"Do we have time to stop and get something to eat? I'm starving."

"Yeah. We should be good."

Outside, Rashawn and I put their suitcases in the trunk, and we piled in, with Aubrielle in the front with me.

"Where y'all wanna eat? We got a little time but not enough to sit down and eat at a restaurant," I told them.

"Why don't we just eat at the airport?" Keyla suggested. "Then we won't have to rush, because we'll already be there."

"That makes sense. Let's do that," Aubrielle agreed.

ONCE WE MADE it through security, we headed toward our gate, figuring we would find a restaurant on the way. Aubrielle and Keyla walked ahead of us while we lagged behind, pulling the suitcases.

"I bet Keyla got some good pussy between them thick ass thighs," Rashawn said low enough that only I could hear him.

"Nigga, that's my woman's cousin. I ain't trying to hear all that."

"My bad, bruh. I tried to convince her to share a room with me. She wouldn't even entertain the idea."

"What's your end goal with her? You just trying to fuck, or…"

"You know me, bruh," he said with a sneaky grin.

I shook my head. "I may be wrong, but Keyla don't seem like the type to put up with that shit you be on."

"I know what I'm doing, Shaad. You know I'm straight up with all the women I deal with. I'll let her know wassup, and if she don't wanna fuck with me, that's cool. We can be friends."

"What about here?" Aubrielle asked, stopping in front of a restaurant called Taylor Gourmet.

"Wherever you wanna eat is cool with me, baby," I told her. It was a bit early to be eating hoagies, but I was smart enough not to share my thoughts.

Once inside, we approached the counter, and each of us ordered our food. Aubrielle chose a table next to the window, and we sat next to each other, leaving the chairs across from us empty for Rashawn and Keyla. After everyone was seated, Aubrielle passed around the hand sanitizer, then we prepared to eat our food.

"Keyla Carson, is that you?"

Everyone looked in the direction of the man's voice.

"Oh my God, Treyvon."

Keyla scooted her seat back before standing and sliding behind Rashawn's chair to get to Treyvon. They hugged each other like old friends.

"I thought that was you. How are you, beautiful?" Treyvon asked when they released each other, but their hands remained connected in front of them.

"I'm good. How are you?"

"I can't complain. Things have gotten a lot better since my brother was released from the hospital."

"How is he?" she asked.

"He's doing well. His physical therapy ended about two months ago. It's been a long, tough journey, but things are looking up for him."

"I'm so glad to hear that. Oh, I'm sorry, Treyvon. This is my cousin, who's more like a sister, Aubrielle, her boyfriend Rashaad, and his brother Rashawn. You guys, this is Treyvon. His brother was a patient of mine after a terrible car accident almost a year ago."

Aubrielle and I greeted Treyvon with a, "Nice to meet you."

Rashawn only gave him a head nod but didn't look up from his food. I had to chuckle at his ass.

"Nice meeting all of you," Treyvon returned. "Where you headed." His attention was back on Keyla.

"My aunt and uncle, Aubrielle's parents, are having a big party for their anniversary, so we're headed to Atlanta."

"No, shit! That's where I'm headed. A friend of mine from college is having a big party for her birthday. Is your number still the same? Maybe we can hook up."

"Yes, Treyvon, my number is still the same. But tell me why I should connect with you while in a whole 'nother state when we haven't connected in all these months right here in D.C?"

He nodded. "You right, and that's my bad. Everything was so hectic with my brother when I brought him home. Before I knew it, too much time had passed, and I didn't think you'd still be interested."

Keyla looked to be thinking about what Treyvon had said and didn't reply immediately.

"My weekend is already packed, but I'll be looking for your call next week."

"A'ight, cool. I'm gon' call this time, for real," he promised.

"The ball is in your court, Treyvon."

They said their goodbyes, and Keyla sat back down and got right to her food. Nobody said anything for a minute or so, then Aubrielle finally said, "Soooo cousin, he's foineee!"

"I know, right!" Keyla agreed. "His ass better call this time."

"The fuck?" Rashawn griped.

"Did you forget I was sitting here, baby?" I asked.

"My bad, baby. You're way finer than him."

She leaned toward me and kissed my cheek. I was satisfied with that answer, but Rashawn's face was still frowned up.

"How you gon' make plans with that nigga like I wasn't right here?" he asked Keyla.

"The same way you replied to all those text messages from your numerous hoes when we were on the way here," she replied before taking a bite of her sandwich.

"That ain't the same. I would've respectfully dismissed their asses if they approached us like he did."

"Rashawn, we are not a couple, okay? Chill out."

"I know we ain't a couple, but he ain't know that."

"He knows now," she said, taking another bite of her sandwich while Rashawn looked pissed.

Aubrielle and I struggled to hold back our laughs but failed. I couldn't believe he was in his feelings after all that shit Rashawn was talking earlier. This was going to be an interesting trip.

15

AUBRIELLE

By the time we landed, it was a little after one in the afternoon. It took us over an hour to get to the hotel from the airport with Atlanta traffic, but we were finally in line waiting to check in.

Rashawn and Keyla were flirting with each other again. He was such a charmer. I knew it was hard for her to stay mad at him. I didn't think it'd be long before she gave in to her attraction for him.

"What's the plan for tonight?" Rashaad asked, standing behind me with his arms around my waist.

"Tonight, the four of us are having dinner at my parents' house, and maybe we'll go to a club or lounge afterward."

"And tomorrow night is your parents' party?"

"Yep. Oh, I forgot to tell you. They decided a few days ago to renew their vows, so the party will be after that."

Everything would take place on Saturday afternoon and evening at the W Hotel in downtown Atlanta, which was also where we were staying.

"Sounds like they're doing it big. Are you excited?"

"I am and a little anxious."

"Why are you anxious?"

I turned around to face him. "Because you're about to meet my parents. Aren't you nervous?"

"Why would I be nervous? I'm a good ass nigga, and there's nothing about me to dislike. If they do, I don't give a fuck, and I mean that in the most respectful way possible, baby. Whether they love me or hate me, you're my woman."

Damn! His words and tone made my pussy moist.

"You good with that?" he asked when I didn't say anything. I was too busy staring at him with googly eyes.

"Ummhmm," I replied with a nod and stood on my toes to kiss his lips.

At the counter, the check-in went smoothly. Keyla and Rashawn had already gone through the process and were waiting for us near the elevators.

"What room are y'all in? I hope y'all not next door to me," Keyla said.

"Why?"

"Because I ain't trying to hear y'all fucking all weekend."

I smacked my lips before saying, "You wrong for that, Key."

She shrugged her shoulders. "I'm just being honest."

"We are not that loud."

"I beg to differ. I mean, I'm glad one of us is getting some, but can you keep it down a little bit?"

I looked at her for a minute to see if she was serious. When she didn't crack a smile, I began to feel guilty for all the loud sex we'd been having.

"My bad, cousin. I'll be more considerate. I had no idea you could hear us."

She maintained a serious expression for several seconds, then said, "Naw, I'm playing with you." She laughed like she'd just told the funniest joke. "Our rooms don't even share walls, and you know I sleep with the fan and my music on. I don't hear shit."

"Damn, Key! You had me feeling guilty. I was about to start looking for my own place when we got back."

She kept laughing at her joke.

"We're in 1207," I told her.

"Oh, good! I'm across the hall in 1206 because I'm sure these walls are paper thin." She continued with her jokes.

"Word?" Rashawn said with a sly grin. "I'm in 1204. I'll keep my side of the adjoining door open just in case you wanna go for a ride."

He adjusted his dick as she looked at him, fighting a smile. Suddenly, she grabbed the handle of her suitcase and began marching toward the front desk.

"Where you going?" I asked.

"To get a different room."

"Aww, hell naw," Rashawn said before going after her.

"I'm not about to deal with these two going back and forth all weekend," I told Rashaad.

"Me either. They need to gon' and fuck and get it over with. Let's go."

I giggled at Rashaad's comment but couldn't agree more. As soon as we got to our very spacious room, Rashaad called his parents to let them know we arrived safely and check on Zara. While he did that, I called my mom to do the same.

"Hey, Ma. We're here and checked in."

"Great! I can't wait to see you girls and meet the man that has swept you off your feet. From the way you talk, he may be my future son-in-law."

"Oh my goodness. You sound like him."

"Really? You two have only been dating a couple of months, and he's already mentioned marriage? Interesting."

"No, Ma. He hasn't said anything about marriage, not in the way you're thinking. He did refer to you and Dad as his in-laws, though."

"Bri, that's the same thing. Men don't play around with marriage. They know right away if you're someone they could marry. From what you've told us about him and the happiness I hear in your voice every time you mention him, I already like him more than Damon's no-good ass."

"Let's not bring him up. Where's Daddy?"

"You know your father. He promised he wouldn't go to the shop today, but that's exactly where he is. He claims he had to get his beard trimmed, but he was supposed to do that yesterday. That man cannot relinquish control for one weekend."

"You know the only way to keep Daddy away from the shop is if you're out of town."

My parents owned and operated Carson's Cuts and More, a combined barbershop and salon, for the past twenty-five years. My mother was a licensed beautician, and my father, a licensed barber.

"I know. I guess there's not a lot that needs to be done. When you told me that Rashaad and his brother were coming, I wanted to have a nice dinner for them, but I refuse to cook this weekend. So dinner for tonight is catered. I hope they don't mind."

"As long as it's good, nobody will mind, Ma. Do you need me and Key to come early and help with anything for tomorrow?"

"Not at all. That's why I hired an event planner, and she is worth every penny."

"Okay then. I'll see you later."

I ended the call and fell back on the bed. Not even thirty seconds later, Rashaad ended his call and was on top of me, using his knees to spread my legs and settling in between them, then planting kisses all over my face.

"Zara wanted to talk to you, but I told her you were taking a nap. She wants you to call her when you wake up," he told me between kisses.

"Why didn't you just let me talk to her?"

"Because all she wants is to ask you who the substitute instructor is for class tomorrow. Once you tell her that, she'll have a million more questions about the instructor. I love Zee, but she asks too many damn questions."

Before I could respond, his lips landed on mine, and while our tongues intertwined, he grinded against me. The thin material of my leggings and his sweats didn't create much of a barrier, and it felt too good to stop him. Rashaad's mouth moved from mine, and he left a trail of kisses as he made his way to my neck. Suddenly, there were a few hard, fast knocks on the door. Of course, he ignored it.

"Baby, the door."

Without acknowledging that he heard me or the knocking at the door, he slid his hand underneath the cropped hoodie I was wearing. This time, the knocking was followed by, "Damn, Bri, y'all fucking already?"

That caused him to stop, and we both broke out in laughter.

"That cousin of yours is a trip," he said, rolling over to the bed.

When I made it to the door, I yanked it open and gave Keyla a dirty look.

"Y'all was fucking for real? We only been here ten minutes."

"If you had knocked five minutes later, your cousin would've been getting her back blown out," Rashaad said.

He had moved over to the other side of the bed, facing the wall, I was sure because of the erection he still had.

"There'll be plenty of time for that. Let's go to Lenox Square," Keyla suggested.

"What's that?" Rashaad asked.

"The mall. You've never heard of it?"

He shook his head. "We can do that. In about thirty to forty-five minutes, we'll meet you downstairs."

"Oh my God. Y'all are just nasty," Keyla said as she turned around to leave.

"That's him, cousin. I'm ready. Rashaad, call your brother and see if he wants to go."

"Elle, are you for real, baby?"

He hopped up from the bed and stopped me from following Keyla into the hallway. His dick print was on full display, causing me to have second thoughts about the mall.

"You gon' leave me like this?" He gripped his dick as if I didn't know what he was talking about.

I struggled to say, "No, because you're coming with me. I'll take care of that before we go to dinner."

"You can't take care of it now *and* before we go to dinner."

"We'll be in the lobby. If you and Rashawn aren't down there in ten minutes, I'll see you when we get back."

Kissing his lips, I left the room quickly before I changed my mind.

～

RASHAAD HAD the nerve to be pouting when they finally made it to the lobby. I pretended like I didn't notice, and by the time we got to the mall, he was in a better mood. After walking around for about twenty minutes, the guys wanted to explore on their own, so we decided to meet at a specific location in an hour.

Before we went our separate ways, Rashaad dug in his pocket and pulled out a wad of cash. Pulling off several bills, he handed them to me and said, "Just in case you see something you like."

"Baby, I have my own money. You—"

"I didn't ask you what you had." He kissed my forehead and walked away.

"Where my money at Rashawn?" Keyla asked with one hand on her hip and the other palm up in the air.

He was walking away and turned around as he dug in his pockets. Just as his brother did, he took out some cash, pulled off some bills, and then placed them in Keyla's hand. Instead of kissing her forehead, he grabbed the back of her neck and crashed his lips onto hers. When he pulled away, he said, "Don't spend it all in one place, baby."

Keyla and I didn't move as we watched them walk away. I was in shock at what I'd just witnessed, and that kiss must have been a doozy because Keyla looked as if she was floating on a cloud.

"Yep! You'll be giving him the pussy before this trip is over. How much did he give you?"

She snapped out of her daze to see how much money was in her hand.

"The fuck? That nigga gave me ten damn singles. I swear I can't stand him!"

I damn near fell out, laughing so hard that tears fell from my eyes and my side began to cramp up.

"Oh my God!" I said through my hysterical laughter.

"Let's go!" she said with an attitude, which caused me to laugh even more.

"You may as well stop fighting it. You know you want that man just as much as he wants you."

"I'm not gon' lie and say I'm not attracted to Rashawn. He's fine as hell and has his shit all the way together. But he's a hoe, Bri, and I don't have time for hoes in my life right now."

"I feel you, but the way he acted at the airport about Treyvon and that kiss he just planted on your lips, he might be feeling you a little more than he's letting on."

"I doubt it. All niggas are territorial, and he probably felt like Treyvon was stepping on his toes."

"What about that kiss?" I asked with raised eyebrows.

She didn't have a response for that but said, "Enough about his ass. Let me find somewhere to spend this measly ten dollars."

We both broke out in laughter again. I was glad Keyla was a good sport about it, but I had a feeling she would be plotting to get him back.

After roaming in and out of a few stores and buying a few things, we found ourselves in Victoria's Secret. As we walked through the store, we ended up separating. I wasn't paying attention to where I was going and ran right into a strong, broad back.

"Oh shoot, I'm sorry. I wasn't—Damon?"

"Bri?"

I had no desire to talk to him, so I attempted to step around his wide body, but he blocked my path. Since he wanted to be an asshole, I turned around and went in the other direction.

"Bri, hold up!" he almost shouted as he came after me. The only reason I slowed my steps was because I didn't want to cause a scene.

"Damon, what do you want? I know you're not in this store alone, and I don't want whoever you came here with in my face talking crazy."

He looked behind him, then back at me before saying, "I haven't seen or talked to you in months. How you—"

"Damon, I was looking—oh shit—Bri—I, umm..."

I couldn't believe my eyes. Standing in front of me, next to my ex-boyfriend, a man I dated for two years and lived with for a year and a half, was someone I considered a friend.

"Really, Niyah?"

"Bri, I—"

"You what? Fucking my ex?"

"Wow!" Keyla exclaimed, appearing out of nowhere. "I told you a long time ago this bitch couldn't be trusted."

"Who you calling a bitch?"

"You, hoe! You call yourself a friend? Probably didn't wait until her side of the bed was cold before you hopped your loose pussy ass in it," Keyla spat.

"Knowing his dirty-dick ass, they were fucking long before I left."

"Excuse me. We're going to have to ask all of you to leave," a sales associate approached us and said.

"Let's go before I snatch this trick up," Keyla threatened as she pulled me by the arm. "I can't stand a disloyal ass bitch. I told you the day I met her ass not to trust her."

Keyla continued to rant as we left the store and moved briskly through the mall. She was walking so fast, I had to grab her shoulder to slow her down.

"Keyla, why you moving so fast? Chill out."

"How can you be so calm about this? That girl been smiling all in your face for years, pretending to be your friend. Then, the first chance she gets, she hooks up with your ex. Hell, they probably were fucking all along, like you said. Bitches like her is why you the only female I trust."

We were approaching the spot where we were meeting the guys, and they were already there waiting. This was not a conversation I wanted to have in front of Rashaad.

"It is what it is, Key. Let's drop it."

I pointed my head in the direction of the guys, and she got my drift. However, she was clearly annoyed, releasing a deep breath and rolling her eyes.

"Fine! But you *waaayy* better than me. I would've snatched that lace front off her head so damn quick. Whew, girl!" She shook her head at the thought.

I'd never in my life fought over a man, and I damn sure wasn't about to fight over a man that was no longer mine. I couldn't care less about who he was fucking. It was Laniyah's actions that had me feeling some kind of way.

16

RASHAAD

As promised, when we got back to our hotel room, Aubrielle gave me some of her good ass pussy. She put it on me so good that I opted not to take a shower with her so I could take a quick nap. When I got out of the shower, she was still naked, sitting on the bed, putting cream all over her body.

My eyes followed her as she went to her suitcase and pulled out a purple pair of panties and bra. I continued to watch as she stepped into her panties and slid them up the lower half of her body and put on her bra. The dark color against her fair skin looked sexy as hell, and I decided to focus on something else because I could feel my dick getting hard. There wasn't enough time to go another round, anyway.

"Have you and Keyla decided where we're going after dinner?" I asked, trying to figure out what I should wear. I wasn't sure if there were strict dress codes in the south. When she didn't answer me after a few long seconds, I called her name.

"Elle?"

"Huh?"

"Are you gon' answer me?"

"Oh, I'm sorry, baby. I was thinking about something. What'd you say?"

"What's on your mind?"

I noticed that she and Keyla were quiet on the way back to the hotel. I planned to ask her what was up, but as soon as we got back to our room, we got busy, and of course, it slipped my mind.

"Nothing important. What did you say?" she repeated.

"We lying to each other now?"

"I'm not lying. It's not important," she said.

"Tell me anyway."

After blowing out a breath, she hesitantly told me about what happened at the mall.

"You and her were good friends?"

She nodded then said, "At least I thought we were, but obviously, I was wrong. Damon doing something like this ain't surprising at all, but I thought Laniyah and I were better than that."

"You think they were fucking around before you and dude broke up?"

"At this point, I wouldn't put it past them. It stung a little when I saw that it was her that he was with, but I'm not gon' lose no sleep over it. I already blocked her number."

"I wish I had some advice for you, baby, but as you've probably noticed, I don't fuck with a lot of people myself. My brother and my uncle the only two niggas I've ever considered friends. Everybody else is an associate."

"That's pretty much how I've always moved, too. I've learned my lesson, though."

Her mood was a little lighter after our conversation, and we proceeded with getting dressed for the evening.

A COUPLE OF HOURS LATER, the Uber driver turned into a long driveway that belonged to a huge house.

"Nice house," I complimented.

"Thank you. This is where we grew up. I thought once Keyla and I left that my parents would downsize, but they said they need all this room for their grandkids."

"They gon' be waiting forever for me to have some kids. I can't even find a man worthy enough to hit it raw," Keyla said.

"You must be blind as hell," Rashawn added. She rolled her eyes at him but didn't say a word.

Once the truck stopped, Rashawn and I got out and helped the girls do the same. My eyes were stuck on Aubrielle, as they had been since she got dressed. She was wearing a pair of very short black shorts with some black heels, and her legs looked so damn good. Underneath the cropped blazer, she wore a bustier that had her titties propped up real nice.

"Baby, I ain't trying to disrespect your parents' house, but I don't know if I can keep my hands off you. You look good as fuck."

"You like what you see, huh?"

She did a little pose, turned around, then twerked her ass cheeks a few times. *She ain't playing fair at all.*

"Keep it up, and I'm gon' have you in your childhood bedroom twerking on my dick."

"Come on before y'all asses be naked in the driveway. Auntie and Uncle cool as hell but not that damn cool," Keyla teased as she led us inside.

"You guys wait here," Aubrielle told Rashawn and I before leaving us in the family room, and her and Keyla disappeared around a corner.

"This shit is nice," Rashawn said, looking around.

"It is. I wonder how much a house this size with this much land costs. I know in D.C. this would be at least a mil."

"Yeah, but we in Georgia, so it was probably half that."

"Who do we have here?" I heard.

Rashawn and I looked in the direction of the woman's voice, and I'll be damned if she didn't look like a slightly older version of Aubrielle. Next to her stood a man who I assumed to be her husband and Aubrielle's father.

"Ma, Dad, this is Rashaad Hanes, the man I've been telling you about, and his brother, Rashawn. These are my parents, Aubrey and Brighton Carson."

When Mrs. Carson extended her hand, I took it and planted a kiss on the back of it after saying, "It's nice to finally meet you."

Mr. Carson waited for me to greet his wife, then extended his hand. I offered a firm handshake and gave him the same verbal greeting. Rashawn politely greeted them both as well.

"Bri, you didn't tell me he was a twin. Key, are you and Rashawn —" Mrs. Carson began.

"No, ma'am. Rashawn and I are *not* dating, Auntie. He just wanted to tag along and be a pest, and they aren't twins."

Mrs. Carson gave Keyla a look before shaking her head and saying, "If you say so, Key. You two would definitely make an attractive couple. I guess I'm wrong on both counts. Do you get mistaken for twins often?" she asked me.

"Not as much as we did when we were growing up, but it still happens occasionally. I'm actually fourteen months older."

"And I'm way better looking, always have been. I don't know how people make that mistake," Rashawn added.

Everyone laughed at Rashawn's humor before Mrs. Carson invited us to the dining room.

"Let's sit and talk before we fill our bellies."

"Does anyone want a drink?" Mr. Carson offered. "The bar is fully stocked."

The girls and Mrs. Carson declined, while Rashawn and I asked for a beer. Mr. Carson disappeared and returned with three Bud Lights. We made our way to the dining room and took our seats. Mr. and Mrs. Carson sat on either end, Aubrielle and I sat on one side, and Keyla and Rashawn sat across from us.

"So Rashaad, my daughter can't seem to talk about anything but you when she calls us these days. I feel like I've known you as long as she has."

"That's good to hear, sir, but if there's anything you want to know about me that she hasn't already told you, feel free to ask."

"There is, actually," he said.

"Daddy, please."

"It's cool, baby," I assured her. She placed her hand on my knee and squeezed.

Her father continued, "The one thing Bri doesn't talk much about is the relationship between you and your daughter's mother. How is it?"

"There's nothing to talk about because there is no relationship," I replied, then took a sip of beer.

"How does that work? Are you involved in our daughter's life?"

"I have full custody of Zara, so I'm very involved. Her mother gave up her parental rights about eight months ago."

"Oh, wow," Mrs. Carson let slip, while her husband didn't have a response. "Bri, you didn't tell us that."

"Look, I appreciate Elle respecting my privacy and not sharing my business with you, but I'm an open book. I ain't got shi—I have nothing to hide."

Aubrielle gave my knee another squeeze. We made eye contact, and she gave me a small smile.

"What caused her to do something so drastic?" Mrs. Carson asked.

"You would have to ask her. I'll be the first to admit that we had a complicated relationship, but we haven't been involved romantically since Zara was a year old. We didn't work."

"I can't think of anything that would push me to such an extreme. There had to be—"

"If you're trying to insinuate that I did something to cause her to take such drastic measures, you couldn't be further from the truth."

"Aye, from day one, my brother has been a damn good father. Zara's mother ain't never been nothing but selfish and self-centered. The best thing she could have ever done for my niece was leave because she didn't know a damn thing about being a good mother," Rashawn interjected.

Everyone was quiet for a moment before Mr. Carson spoke again.

"I appreciate your honesty. I'm sure it was—still is a tough situation."

"It is for my daughter, but we're handling it. My family is very supportive, as you can see." I nodded my head toward my brother.

"Rashaad, I didn't mean to insinuate anything, and I apologize if it seemed that way," Mrs. Carson said.

"No apology needed. I understand how hard it is to wrap your mind around it."

"Well, I think that's enough serious talk for now. Y'all ready to eat?"

I was thankful that Mrs. Carson was ready to change the subject. I didn't mind being in the hot seat, but talking about Carmen still pissed me off.

17

AUBRIELLE

With the way the evening started, I was a little nervous about how dinner would go. To my surprise, once we began to eat and the wine started to flow, everyone relaxed. By everyone, I mean my parents. I had no idea they would question Rashaad about his relationship with Zara's mother, but Rashaad handled it like a champ.

About halfway through dinner, the conversation between my father, Rashaad, and Rashawn flowed so effortlessly one would have never believed that there was some tension less than an hour ago. They were talking about everything from politics to sports and everything in between. After listening to them go back and forth about the Falcons and the Redskins, I turned to look at my mother, and she reached for my hand and gave it a reassuring squeeze. I guess that meant Rashaad had her stamp of approval.

Since the men were deep in their conversation, my mother, Keyla, and I struck up our own.

"Keyla, tell me what's keeping you from snatching this one up," Ma said, nodding her head toward Rashawn.

She looked in his direction, then back at my mother before she answered. "Auntie, I'm gon' tell you like I told Bri. He's a hoe, and I don't have time for those types of problems. Unfortunately, he's not as mature as his brother."

"I don't know, Key. He may need the right woman to tame him. I've been watching the way he looks at you. I think there's something there."

"That's what I told her, Ma."

"Yeah, there is. He wants what's between my legs, and I'm not giving it to him."

"The lies!" I blurted out.

Keyla gasped. "Cousin, don't do that! You're supposed to be on my side, praying for my strength to resist the temptation of the devil."

"Who's the devil?" Rashawn said.

We were so caught up in our conversation that we didn't notice that the guys were listening.

"No one. Y'all ready to hit the club? I'm gonna use the bathroom. Bri, get the Uber."

Keyla pushed away from the table, stood, and was gone. I pulled out my phone and looked at the Uber app to see if there was one close by.

"There's one twenty minutes away. That's enough time to give you guys a quick tour of the house and freshen up."

ONE THING I didn't miss about Atlanta was the traffic. What should have been a thirty-minute ride, took over an hour.

When we pulled up at Josephine Restaurant and Lounge, it was close to eleven, and there was a long line outside. Luckily, I called ahead and reserved a table, which also meant we didn't have to wait in line, because our names were put on a list.

As soon as we were seated, the half-naked bottle girls appeared. The table reservation required that we order a bottle of something. Keyla and I didn't drink hard liquor, so we let the guys handle that while we went to the bathroom.

"Baby, we'll be right back."

I was about to walk away, but he grabbed my hand.

"Gimme a kiss," he demanded when

"Gladly," I replied with a smile.

He released his hold on me after our lips connected. When I turned to walk away, he slapped my ass, startling me and causing me to jump. I gave him a dirty look while he returned a smirk.

Keyla and I moved through the crowded lounge and made our way to the bathroom. I didn't need to use it, so I took some selfies in the full-length mirror while she handled her business.

"Did you tell Auntie about your friend?" Keyla asked while she washed her hands.

"Sure didn't. I told Rashaad, and that's all the energy I want to give to the situation. Damon ain't worth a damn, but if that's who she wants, go 'head, sis."

"I'm glad one of us is mature because I know I wouldn't have handled that well. Damon ain't your man, but it's the principle of it all."

"Yeah, but I'm over it."

On our way back to the table, Keyla led the way. Suddenly, I ran into her back, and when I saw the reason why, I began to wonder if he was the reason Keyla suggested we come here. I couldn't hear their conversation, so I wasn't able to confirm my suspicions. I tapped her shoulder and nodded in the direction of our table, letting her know that was where I'd be.

Of course, when I got back to the guys, they were wondering where Keyla was. Rashawn was the one to ask.

"Where's your cousin?"

"She ran into someone she knew," was all I said.

All he did was nod in response. Rashaad pulled me down to his lap and put his arms around my waist, then said, "Dinner was interesting."

"It sure started that way. I didn't realize that you having a child was a concern of theirs."

"I can understand why. People that have kids together sometimes go back and forth with each other for years before they finally cut each other off permanently, if ever. They were just trying to protect you."

"I guess. It seems like once that conversation was over, y'all got along pretty well."

"We did. Your pops is cool, so is your mom."

The four glasses of wine that I drank at my parents' house and the music the DJ was playing started to get to me. When I started winding my hips on Rashaad's lap, he asked if I wanted to dance.

I'm a dance instructor. Of course, I wanna dance.

Instead of a verbal reply, I got up and led him to the dance floor. The DJ transitioned into "Heat" by Chris Brown and Gunna as we found an open spot on the floor.

"Can you dance without skates?" I teased.

"Skates or not, your man is smooth on his feet."

Although I was the dance instructor, I followed his lead. He took me by the hand, spun me around, then pulled my body against his. Chest to chest, we swayed from left to right on tempo with the beat. I mirrored his every move, and each time our bodies disconnected, although it would only be for milliseconds, I longed to get back to him. The way he looked at me was so intense I was mesmerized, and it felt as if I was melting under his gaze.

As the song ended, my back was against his chest, and his erection massaged my ass cheeks. I closed my eyes and let my head fall back on his shoulder, giving him access to my neck, of which he took full advantage. His lips against my skin felt heavenly, causing my panties to become damp and my mind to get lost in the sensations. As one of his hands rubbed up and down my thigh, the other made its way to my breasts. Only God knows what I would have let him do to me on that dance floor but leave it to Keyla to ruin the mood.

"Y'all just gon' fuck right here on the dance floor?"

I opened my eyes, and there was Keyla with a sneaky grin on her face and Treyvon standing behind her.

"Whatever, heffa. Good to see you again, Treyvon."

Rashaad spoke to Treyvon, and on our way back to our table, he said, "That's the friend she ran into?"

I nodded. "And I don't know if he's the reason she suggested we come here, so don't ask."

"It looks like Shawn is occupied anyway." He tilted his head in the direction of our table.

That he was, with a thick, brown-skinned beauty sitting on his lap. When Rashaad and I sat down, his brother didn't notice us, because he was so wrapped up in his new friend. While we were gone, a bottle of white wine had been delivered, along with a bottle of Hennessy. After pouring me a glass of wine and himself some Hennessy, we sat back and chilled, watching the crowd. About five minutes passed before Rashawn realized we'd come back.

"How long y'all been here?" he asked.

"A few minutes. Who's your friend?" I asked.

"Oh, shit. My bad. This is…"

"Thomasina."

"That's right. This is Thomasina. Thomasina, this is my brother, Rashaad, and his girl, Aubrielle."

"Oh my God! Are you guys twins?" Thomasina asked with excitement.

"No, we're not twins. He's my older brother."

"Aww, that's too bad. I've always wanted to hook up twins."

Hold up! Did this hoe not just hear Rashawn introduce me as Rashaad's girl?

Just as I was about to address what she said, Keyla and Treyvon approached the table.

"Oh, it looks like we have a guest," Keyla said with her eyes on Thomasina.

"Looks like we have two. What's your name again, bruh?"

Surprisingly, Rashawn stuck his hand out for Treyvon, who gave him a firm shake as he leaned in and said his name.

"Treyvon and some of his frat brothers are here hanging out. They have a nice-sized VIP section with plenty of open space, and he invited us up. Y'all wanna go?"

Before any of us could say anything, Thomasina was on her feet, answering for all of us.

"Yes! That sounds like fun. Let's go, Shawn."

I questioned Rashaad with my eyes, and he shrugged his shoulders, indicating that he was cool with it. I couldn't read his brother's expression, but I had a feeling that going to a VIP section with Treyvon and his frat brothers was the last thing Rashawn wanted to do.

18

RASHAAD

We got up to the VIP section, and there were a nice amount of people in the space, and as Keyla said, it was spacious. Although I didn't go to a four-year university, I was familiar with all of the Black Greek organizations. With all the purple and gold on display, it didn't take a rocket scientist to know which fraternity Treyvon belonged to.

Treyvon introduced us to a few of his frat brothers, and we found a place to sit. We brought our drinks with us, but with the way the liquor was flowing up there, we could have left our bottles for the group Aubrielle graciously offered our table.

Thomasina had gotten comfortable on Rashawn's lap again. As she tried to hold a conversation with him, his eyes were focused on Keyla, who was sitting next to Treyvon, sneaking glances at Rashawn.

"This shit is crazy."

"If you're talking about your brother and my cousin, I agree. I can't wait to get Keyla alone so I can ask her if she planned this."

"You think she's trying to make Shawn jealous?"

"Probably, but they aren't our problem. Let's dance."

"Naw, let's not. You had my dick hard as fuck out there. I forgot where we were for a minute."

She laughed, but I was serious as hell. Had Keyla not interrupted us, wasn't no telling how far I would have tried to go.

"Well, I wanna dance. I'm gonna see if Keyla wants to."

"What about Thomasina?" I joked.

"Don't play with me, Rashaad. I still wanna pop her ass in her mouth for that slick comment she made."

She went to stand, but I held her down.

"Elle, don't be out there shaking ya ass and shit. I'm outnumbered, but I will fuck all these niggas up."

"Okay." She tried to get up again, but I wasn't done.

"What, Rashaad?"

I gripped the back of her neck and brought her face within an inch of mine.

"Gimme a kiss."

Our mouths met in a short but passionate lip-lock, and this time, when she tried to get up, I let her go, tapping that ass before she got too far away.

I sat back with my drink and watched my woman walk a few feet away to where Keyla was seated. Without asking, she pulled Keyla to her feet and to the area where a few others were dancing. As if Aubrielle had planned it, "Cash Money Records taking over for the '99 and the 2000," boomed through the speakers, and every female in VIP, including Aubrielle, lost their damn minds. The dance floor was now filled with ass and titties. Thomasina hopped off Rashawn's lap as well, and he slid a little closer to me.

"What is it with females and this damn song?" Rashawn asked.

"I don't know, but I told Elle not to be out there shaking her ass."

"Man, you can hang that up. She's definitely out there shaking her ass."

"Naw, I doubt it."

"Women can't control themselves when 'Back That Azz Up' comes on, bruh. Did you not see how they just rushed the floor?"

I looked toward the crowd of women and noticed a few men had joined, and they'd formed a circle around someone. I couldn't see who was in the middle, but when I looked around the perimeter, I didn't see Aubrielle.

Rashawn peeped what I was looking at and said, "I guarantee your girl is in the center of that circle turnt the fuck up."

Against my better judgment, I went over to see what everyone was looking at, with my brother right behind me. When we maneuvered our way to the front, I was only a little surprised that Rashawn was right. Aubrielle was in the center, and all eyes were on her as she performed a sexy ass routine to the old-school track. I couldn't even be mad, because she was in her element, and the way she moved was a thing of beauty.

The only time I'd ever seen Aubrielle dance was when she was instructing Zara's class or on skates. This was very different from that, and I was more than impressed with her skills. Yes, some ass shaking was going on, but the way she did it was different from the average woman twerking in a club, and that was only a small part of her routine. Almost everyone in VIP was recording her, and I was sure before we left the club, she'd be all over social media.

When the DJ started to blend in "Hey Ladies" by Travis Porter, Aubrielle's eyes landed on me, and her lips curled into a big smile. She gestured "come here" with her index finger, and before another nigga thought she was talking to him, I went to my woman, and she proceeded to shake her ass and twerk all over my pelvic area. That wasn't as interesting as her kicking her legs above her head and doing the splits to Juvenile, so the small crowd began to disperse.

By the time that song ended, my dick was hard, and I was ready to call it a night. After looking at my watch, I decided we'd stay a little bit longer since it wasn't even twelve thirty.

"I need some water," Aubrielle said once we were back at our seats.

"I bet you do. I thought I told you not to be out there shaking your ass."

"My bad, baby, but I have no control over my body when certain songs come on, and that's one of them."

"I tell you what, if you can do the splits on my dick like you did out there on the dance floor, all is forgiven."

She gasped and pushed my shoulder but didn't give me an answer.

"I'm serious, Elle. That shit was amazing."

"I guess I can do that for you."

"Word?" She nodded. "Get the Uber. It's time to go," I told her. "Aye, bruh, we about to head out. You ready?" I asked Rashawn, interrupting the conversation he was having with Thomasina.

He looked over at Keyla, then said, "Naw, I think I'm gon' chill a lil' longer."

"A'ight, cool." I turned back to Aubrielle. "Shawn ain't ready. Did you tell Keyla we were leaving?"

"No, Rashaad. It's been three seconds. Calm down, baby. This pussy ain't going nowhere."

She got up to let Keyla know that we were leaving. They talked for a few minutes before she came back and we said our goodbyes and left. The Uber had arrived by the time we got outside, and like some horny ass teenagers, we made out for the entire ride to the hotel.

19

AUBRIELLE

The next morning, I was awakened by constant vibrating. I opened my eyes, just barely, and the sun almost blinded me. Closing the blinds was the last thing on our minds when we got to our room. All we wanted to do was relieve the throbbing of our genitals.

My head was pounding from too much wine, and my body ached from too much Rashaad, who was sleeping peacefully next to me. The vibrating continued, and it sounded like it was above my head, so I reached up and felt around the nightstand. Since I didn't look at the screen, I didn't realize that it was Rashaad's phone, and I answered a FaceTime call from Zara.

"Hello," I said, voice heavily laced with sleep.

"Ms. Aubrielle?" Zara said.

"Oh," I opened my eyes a little more and made sure the comforter was pulled up to my neck. "Hey, sweetheart. Why are you up so early?"

"It's not that early. I just got back from dance class. I didn't like our teacher today. She wasn't nice like you."

"Aww, I'm sorry. I'll be back for class on Monday. Did you still pay attention?"

"Yes, ma'am. How come you answered my daddy's phone? Is he with you?"

"Oh, umm—he—yes, he's—"

"Is that my daddy? Is he sleeping in the bed with you?"

"Zara, umm, let me call you back, sweetie."

I ended the call without waiting for her to respond and let out a deep breath.

"You could have just told her lil' nosy ass the truth," Rashaad said. When I looked at him, his eyes were still closed.

"Why didn't you say something?"

"Because I wanted to see what you would say. I'm not sure what you're trying to hide. Her mother is the only woman she's ever seen me with, and it wasn't in a romantic way. Zara knows you're my woman."

He turned away from me and dug himself deeper into the bed.

"That doesn't mean she has to know we sleep in the same bed. I don't want to be a negative influence on her."

He turned just his head toward me and opened his eyes.

"Us being in the same bed might be strange to her but only because me and her mom had separate rooms. That's probably why she asked. It's not as big a deal as you're making it out to be. What time is it?"

I looked at his phone that I was still holding. "Nine thirty."

"What time everything start today?"

"Not until five."

"Good. Close the blinds. I'm going back to sleep."

He turned away from me and was softly snoring before I was able to ease out of bed. I could guarantee that my flexibility was better than the average thirty-four-year-old woman, but last night, Rashaad had me in positions that defied gravity and physics. I made it over to the window and pulled the blinds closed, then found the extra-strength Tylenol in my suitcase and took two of them before going back to bed.

The next time I opened my eyes, Rashaad's side of the bed was empty. It didn't sound like anyone was in the bathroom, so I assumed he stepped out. After staring at the ceiling for a few minutes, I slowly got out of bed and moved around the room, searching for my purse, where I believed my phone was located.

When I found it, there was a text from Rashaad that said he went to get food.

"Damn, I can't believe I slept this late," I said to myself when I saw that it was twelve twenty.

After using the bathroom, I wrapped myself in the robe that the hotel supplied, washed my face, brushed my teeth, and put my hair into a low ponytail because it was all over my head. Back in the bedroom, Rashaad had returned and was sitting on the couch behind the coffee table, pulling food out of a bag.

"Oh my goodness. How'd you get Atlanta Breakfast Club?" I asked when I saw the name of the restaurant on the bag.

"Uber Eats."

"Their food is so good. How'd you even know about them?"

"I know how to use Google, baby. I got you the peach cobbler French toast and me the breakfast bowl."

"Yes!" I cheered.

I was so hungry that I forgot how sore I was, but when I moved to sit next to him on the couch, my body reminded me. My expression showed my mild discomfort, and of course, the person who caused it took notice.

He grinned before leaning in and placing a soft kiss on my lips. Then he said, "You good, baby? Looks like you moving kinda slow."

"You should not be poking fun at the pain you caused."

"I would offer to poke something else, but that seems to be the reason you're in this predicament." He laughed.

"It's not funny, Rashaad. We'll see how much laughing you do when I withhold the pussy," I warned.

"Don't play with me, Elle," he warned back.

"Who's playing? My entire body has never been sore from just sex."

"That's where you got it mixed up, baby. What we do is beyond sex. We on some next level shit."

"If you say so."

"I know so," he said confidently.

We quietly prepped our food, and when I ate the first mouthful, I closed my eyes, let my head fall back, and moaned as I savored the delicious peach cobbler flavor.

"This is heavenly. Thank you so much, baby." I stuffed another forkful in my mouth.

"Anything for you, Elle. This is good, too."

"Let me taste."

"You haven't even put a dent in your food. Why you wanna try mine?"

"'Cause it looks good. Just a little bit."

He released a deep breath as he prepared to give me a forkful. "You're lucky I love your ass because I don't like sharing my food. I don't even share with Zara."

I looked at him to see if he realized what he said, but when he lifted the fork to my mouth to feed me without missing a beat, I figured he didn't.

"Mmm, that's good, too. Here, try mine."

I lifted a piece to his mouth with my fork and fed it to him.

"Damn! That tastes just like peach cobbler."

"I know! It's like having dessert for breakfast."

We enjoyed our food in silence for a few minutes before I said, "I wonder what time Key and Shawn got in last night and if they had company."

"I talked to Shawn for a minute while I waited for the food. Sounded like he was still knocked out, but I guarantee you he ain't let Keyla bring that nigga back to her room."

"Keyla is not his woman, so he can't control what she does."

"How much you wanna bet?" he asked with a sly grin.

"I'm not betting you, because you probably just wanna fuck while I'm in a headstand or some shit as your reward."

"We did that this morning," he joked.

I gasped. "We did not, and we never will. I'll do some freaky shit, but I'm not doing no damn headstand, Rashaad."

"I'm just playing with your freaky ass. It don't matter what position we in. The pussy is always good."

He gave me another kiss just as his phone began to vibrate, and Zara's face popped up on the screen.

"This is exactly why she didn't need a cell phone. I can't believe I let Sheeda talk me into getting a six-year-old a damn iPhone. Hey, baby girl." I laughed at how he switched right into daddy mode.

"Daddy, Ms. Aubrielle said she was gonna call me back, and she didn't call back yet."

"That's because it was early, and she went back to sleep."

"Did you sleep in the same bed with her like Gigi and Pop-Pop?"

He looked at me, and I shook my head, begging him with my eyes not to tell her. He was hesitant but proceeded to say, "Zee, you are too young to be asking so many questions. How was dance class?"

"It was good, but I didn't like the teacher. She was mean. I told Ms. Aubrielle when I called you this morning because she answered your phone."

Ignoring her comment, he said, "We'll be back Monday morning, so you won't have that instructor again. Are you being good for Gigi and Pop-Pop?"

"I'm always good, Daddy. Can I talk to Ms. Aubrielle now?"

"No, Zee. Ms. Aubrielle had to run some errands. I'll have her call you when she gets a chance."

"Okay, Daddy. I love you. Tell Ms. Aubrielle I love her, too. I can see her in the window sitting by you. Bye, Daddy."

Zara ended the call before Rashaad could respond, and we looked at each other and fell out laughing.

"Who the hell am I raising?"

"I don't know, but she's too smart for her own good. It's gonna be hard to hide things from her."

"That's why I keep telling your scary ass we don't need to hide nothing from her."

"You trying to play house, and I think it's too soon for all that. Zara has been through a lot, and if things don't work out—"

"Why are you thinking about us not working out? I don't like that shit."

"I want us to work, Rashaad. Right now, I can't imagine my life without you, but things happen, and the last thing I want to do is hurt Zara."

"Baby, if we want us to work, we will. Don't let seeds of doubt plant themselves in your mind, because eventually, they'll start to manifest. Every morning when I wake up, one of my main goals is to do whatever I can to earn a permanent place in your heart. Stop saying and thinking that negative shit when it comes to us or anything else. Positivity breeds positivity. Okay?"

I nodded.

"Naw, I need to hear that you understand what I'm saying, Elle."

"I hear you."

"Good. For the record, I'm not trying to play house with you. I want to make a home. Whenever you're ready."

20

RASHAAD

When we finished eating, I told Aubrielle that I had a surprise for her and to put on something comfortable.

"Are we going somewhere because I need to shower?"

"Yes, we are, and you don't need to shower. Hurry up!" I slapped her on her ass to hurry her along.

"Rashaad, after everything we did last night, I *need* to shower. I can't go any outside with dry semen everywhere."

She had a point. I looked at my watch, and we had about twenty minutes to get down to the spa. I knew she'd be sore after everything we did last night, so while I was waiting for the food, I made her an appointment.

"You got ten minutes. If you take any longer than that, we'll be late."

She hurried into the bathroom while I waited. Aubrielle wasn't very high maintenance. She was naturally beautiful and didn't wear a lot of makeup when she wore it. Her attire was mostly leggings and oversized sweatshirts or hoodies because she taught dance almost every day. Ten minutes later, she appeared in a pair of running shorts, a fitted T-shirt, and a pair of Nike slides.

"I'm ready."

In the hallway, I took her hand and led her to the elevator.

"You haven't heard from Keyla?"

"She sent a text saying she was hungover, and she'd see me at the party."

"She must have drunk something else after we left. Wine shouldn't have her hungover like that."

"Wine will sneak up on you. I had to take some Tylenol this morning because my head was pounding. Keyla was out longer than I was, so she probably drank more than I did. Hell, maybe she did drink something else."

It took less than a minute to get to the sixteenth floor, where the spa was located. When Aubrielle saw where I was taking her, she turned to me with a big smile on her face.

"Aww, baby, this is so sweet," she cooed as we entered.

She wrapped her arms around my torso, resting her head on my chest as she hugged me tightly.

"I haven't been able to spoil you very much since we've been together, and I wanted to do a little something to show you that I appreciate having you in my life."

"You're so sweet. Are you joining me?"

"No, but I'll stay and keep you company if you want."

"I want you to stay and have done whatever I'm having done. It'll be fun."

"Elle, I booked you the works, and I'm not about to get a manicure or pedicure or no damn facial."

"Men get all of that all the time," the woman waiting to greet us said. "It's not uncommon, sir."

Aubrielle looked at me with her lip poked out and pleading eyes.

"Fine! But don't have my nails looking glossy when we leave here."

We spent the next few hours in the spa getting pampered. Everything was cool, but the massage was what I enjoyed most. By the time we returned to our room, we had just enough time to get ready for the party.

When I stepped out of the bathroom after taking a shower, Aubrielle was sitting in front of the vanity area that was right outside of the door, putting the finishing touches on her hair. Her makeup was already done, and although I still preferred her bare face or maybe a small amount of makeup for every day, I had to admit, she looked good as fuck.

We'd had dinner at a few nice restaurants in D.C., but this was the first time since we'd been together that we had the opportunity to get dressed up, and I was looking forward to seeing her in the little dark-orange dress she had hanging on the door. I smiled as I watched her put the finishing touches on her hair. At the moment, all she had on was a matching black panty and bra set. Aubrielle was petite and curvier than most would expect a dancer to be, but her body was perfect to me. *She* was perfect to me.

When she caught me staring at her in the mirror, she smiled and turned around to face me.

"Why are you staring and smiling at me?"

"Because I was imagining our future together, and what I saw made me smile."

"What'd you see?" she asked, taking a few steps toward me and reaching for my hands.

"I think I'm falling in love with you."

I didn't mean to say that.

"You—You—"

"Actually, I'm sure I'm already in love with you."

That either.

"How—How can you be so sure?"

"Because you're the only woman that I've ever imagined a future with. Because I miss you as soon as you walk away, and I think about you the whole time we're apart. Because being with you is the easiest thing I've ever done and the only thing that makes sense."

I hadn't planned to say any of that, because it wasn't until that moment that I realized I was in love with Aubrielle. Her eyes became a little watery, but the smile on her face assured me that any tears that fell would be happy tears.

"You're gonna make me mess up my makeup," she said.

"My bad, baby. I didn't—"

"No, no, it's fine. You're just—I don't even know what I'm trying to say."

She released my hands and walked back toward the vanity. After pulling a few tissues from the box, she dabbed her eyes as she sat on the edge of the bed.

"Earlier today, when we were eating breakfast, you said you loved me."

I thought back to that time and couldn't recall saying those words.

"I figured you didn't know what you said, and I thought it was just a slip of the tongue."

Sitting next to her, I said, "It may have been my subconscious mind admitting what my conscious mind hadn't quite realized. Elle, I'm not trying to pressure you or rush you to feel the same way. You—"

"What? No, that's not it, at all. Being with you has felt right since the moment you first put your hands on my waist. I didn't know who you were or what you looked like, but I felt like in your arms was where I belonged. Every moment I've spent with you since, that feeling has only magnified. You're not pressuring me or rushing me to feel a certain way because the feelings have been there. I'm already in love with you."

"My spirit has never been more at peace than it's been since I laid eyes on you. You're what's been missing from my life. I need you to trust me with your heart, Elle. I know you've given it to some undeserving ass niggas before, but I'm not them."

"I know. It's just—"

I shook my head, and she stopped talking midsentence.

"I meant it when I said no more negative thoughts. Whatever you were about to say was gon' fuck up this special moment. The moment we confessed our true feelings for each other, and I can't let you do that, Elle. Do you believe me when I say I love you?"

"Yes, I believe you. I love you, too."

"Damn, baby. Hearing that makes me wanna skip this dinner and spend the rest of the night making love to you."

Leaning forward, I kissed her softly but didn't dare let my lips linger on her for too long. I knew if I did, we'd miss tonight's festivities, and I didn't want to be the cause of that.

21

AUBRIELLE

The event space where the festivities would be held was decorated beautifully in shades of burnt oranges, golds, and browns. Keyla and I left Rashaad and Rashawn there while we went to my parents' suite to see if they needed any assistance.

"Aren't y'all supposed to be in different rooms or something? The groom isn't supposed to see the bride before the wedding," I said when we walked in.

"Bri, we've been married for thirty-five years. I know what my wife looks like," Daddy said.

"You still could have been surprised for today," Keyla added.

"If we had thought about renewing our vows sooner, maybe we would have gone the traditional route. However, he was with me when I found the dress and has seen me in it half a dozen times when I was getting the alterations."

"And you look damn good, baby. I can't wait to get you back up here so I can—"

"Aht, aht! You will not talk nasty in front of the children," I said, waving my hands in the air.

"Children?" My mother sashayed over to us in her floor-length gold dress and burnt-orange accessories. "What were *you* doing last night? That makeup doesn't cover up all those marks Rashaad left on your neck."

I gasped, putting my hands over my neck, then rushed to the nearest mirror to see if the hickeys that Rashaad marked me with were visible. I could have sworn I covered them up.

"And don't try to act like you're Miss Innocent," Ma said to Keyla. "You may not have marks on your neck, but you're glowing. Did you give in to that handsome Rashawn?"

"What? I—Auntie—Why are you asking me that?" Keyla stammered over her words.

"A simple yes or no will do, Key."

"Keyla Renee Carson, did you hook up with Rashawn?"

"Did y'all forget I was in this room? I don't care how old y'all are. I don't wanna hear none of this shit. What did y'all come up here for anyway?" Daddy said with a look of dismay on his face.

"Nothing. Let's go, Bri. We'll see y'all downstairs."

Before another word could be spoken, Keyla dragged me out of the room. She must have forgotten I was wearing heels or something the way she was pulling me. When we got in the hallway, I steadied myself on my feet and yanked my arm away from her.

"You did it, didn't you?"

Hesitating briefly, she confessed, "I did, Bri, and it was *the* absolute best sex I've ever had in my life. I can't even put it into words."

"I guess him and his brother have that in common. So that hangover story was a lie?"

"Girl, he was so deep inside me when I sent that text, but I had to reply because I didn't want you to come knocking on the door."

"Damn! I knew it would happen sooner or later, but I had some doubts when you met up with Treyvon. Did you plan that?"

"I mean, he texted me and said he and his frat brothers were gonna be there, and since we were looking for something to do, I figured, why not?"

"Were you trying to make Rashawn jealous?" I whispered. We were right outside of the event space, and I didn't want to be overheard.

"Maybe a little."

"Looks like it worked."

"I have one little problem, though," she whispered.

"What?"

"I invited Treyvon to come here later. His friend's party is a day party, and it'll be over at like six or something."

"Keyla! What are you gonna do?"

"I don't know what to do. Rashawn and I haven't defined anything, so technically, we aren't together."

"Are you crazy? Even if y'all not official, he ain't gon' be happy about Treyvon showing up here. You better text him and tell him not to come."

Before she could reply, the doors opened, and Rashaad and Rashawn walked out, both looking as fine as ever. Rashaad was wearing a pair of chocolate-colored slacks with a button-down dress shirt that was the same shade of orange as my dress. Rashawn was wearing a pair of black slacks with a pale-yellow dress shirt.

"People are starting to arrive, and we didn't know where to sit," Rashaad told me.

"It's not that formal, but I wanna be up close."

I took his hand, and the four of us went inside. The event planner was milling around, checking on everything. The space was set up banquet style with several round tables. The dance floor was in the front of the room with the DJ stationed nearby on a riser.

The four of us sat at a table near the dance floor. Keyla and I were next to each other, and the guys were on either side of us. We spoke to our relatives and family friends as they arrived. When our cousin Deena sat down across from us, Keyla and I gave each other a knowing look and rolled our eyes. We stopped dealing with Deena when we were teenagers after she had sex with a guy that Keyla was dating.

Keyla didn't hold on to her virginity as long as I did, but she was a virgin when she was dating Dwight. Deena knew that Keyla wasn't giving it up and talked that nigga right out of his drawers. He was extremely remorseful afterward and ended up confessing to Keyla. Of course, she still broke up with him, and from then on, we were done with Deena. She was probably the messiest individual I'd ever had the displeasure of knowing.

"Hey, cousins," she greeted us with phony excitement.

"Aren't there some empty seats at another table?" I asked.

"Damn, Bri. It's like that?"

"It's been like that for years, Dee," Keyla reminded her.

She kissed her teeth and put her focus on the two men at the table.

"Anyway...some people have no manners. I'm Deena, their irresistible cousin."

She leaned forward, exposing her already very visible cleavage, and extended her hand toward the middle of the table. When Rashaad began to lift his arm to shake her hand, I punched him in his bicep.

"Ouch, Elle! I'm just trying to be polite," Rashaad said, rubbing his arm, knowing damn well I didn't hit him that hard.

Rashawn just nodded his head in Deena's direction, leaving her hand hanging in the air.

"Well, shit! Where y'all find these fine ass niggas at? I know they ain't from the A."

"Why? Because you ain't fucked them yet?" Keyla said.

"Damn, Key! That shit happened so long ago. It's not like you was gon' marry the nigga. Let bygones be bygones, cousin. It's time to kiss and make up."

"Deena, if you don't take your messy ass to another table. You know we don't fuck with you like that, and we never will," I said, trying to intervene before Keyla's hotheaded ass went off.

"Y'all sure can hold on to a grudge. Some things never change, I see."

"Neither do some people. You still a hoe, right?" Keyla's mouth had always been lethal.

"Aye, I don't even know you, but you done fucked up the whole vibe over here. Take your ass on somewhere," Rashawn said.

Deena was used to getting her way with men, so Rashawn's words took her by surprise. She frowned up her face, stood up in a huff, then stomped away.

"Wassup with her?" Rashaad asked.

"I'll tell you later. It's about to start."

THE SHORT CEREMONY WAS BEAUTIFUL. When it was time to recite their vows, my parents spoke from the heart, and their words had me in tears. I'd always dreamed of having a love like theirs, and I might have had to kiss a few frogs along the way, but I believed I'd finally found my king. During the ceremony, Rashaad held my hand, and I felt his gaze on me for almost the whole ceremony. A few times, he lifted it to his lips and left soft kisses on the back of it. My heart was beyond full by the time my parents said, "I do, again".

Dinner was over, and the reception was in full swing. The DJ played a little something for everybody, but he mostly rocked the hits from the eighties since those songs were popular when my parents and many of their guests were in their twenties. My love for dance definitely came from Aubrey and Brighton. They hadn't left the dance floor since dinner ended, and I could have watched them enjoy each other all night.

"Oh, shit!" Keyla exclaimed, dropping the drink she'd just gotten from the bar.

I followed her line of vision, and my eyes got wide.

"Key! You were supposed to tell him not to come."

"I know, but it slipped my mind when everything started. Shit! Shit! Shit!"

"The guys went up to Rashawn's room to get some liquor because he said the stuff from the bar was weak. I'll run interference while you get rid of him. Hurry up!"

I hurried into the hallway and rounded the corner. When I got close to the elevators, I heard a familiar and unwelcome voice calling me. I slowly turned around and became infuriated with the sight before me.

"Why are you here?"

"I was invited."

"You were uninvited. Goodbye!"

"I need to ex—"

"No, you don't. I'm good on you." I turned back toward the elevators.

"Wait, Bri. Please."

I whipped back around angrily. "What the fuck do you want, Laniyah?"

"Me and Damon didn't happen until after you left."

"Is that supposed to make it better?"

"I just need you to know that nothing ever happened between us while you were together. You know me better than anybody, and you know I wouldn't do that to you?"

"Is that all?"

"Bri, please. You're happy with your new life and new man. Why can't you be happy for me?"

"Do you hear yourself? You're claiming to be happy with the man who claimed to be in love with your 'friend' but broke her heart repeatedly by cheating on her multiple times. Make it make sense, Niyah."

"He's different now. You leaving him was the wake-up call he needed to get his shit together. I figured since you moved on—"

Something in me snapped and before I could stop myself, the palm of my hand went across her cheek. Her head flung to the left and she reached up and touched her face. Her expression was one of disbelief.

"You're right, I have moved on, and I'm madly in love with Rashaad. I wish you and Damon nothing but happiness but me and you…we can't be friends."

I spun on my heels and confidently walked toward the elevators. This time, I ignored her calling my name. When I pushed the button to go up, the elevator doors opened, and Rashaad and Rashawn stepped off.

"Hey, baby. You look upset. Did something happen?" Rashaad asked.

"Ain't nothing wrong with her," Rashawn said before I could reply, shaking his head. "She act like she can't be away from your ass for ten minutes before withdrawal sets in."

"Shut your hating ass up. You mad 'cause don't nobody miss your ass when you gone," Rashaad threw back at him.

As we walked back toward the party, Rashaad said, "We called Rasheeda to check on RBL. She finally answered," he told me.

"Is everything good?"

"From what she said, everything's cool. I haven't heard anything different from my Pops or Barry."

"That's good," I said absently.

My mind was still on my conversation with Laniyah until my eyes landed on Keyla and Treyvon walking toward the exit.

"Oh, damn," I said under my breath.

"Aww, shit!" Rashaad said.

"Keyla!" Rashawn shouted.

She and Treyvon looked in our direction, but Keyla quickly looked away and began pushing Treyvon through the doors. Rashawn was taking long strides that way, leaving me and Rashaad behind.

"What's up with that? I know she told you what happened with her and Shawn."

"She did, but she invited Treyvon to come tonight before all that. I told her to uninvite him, but said she forgot. Rashawn ain't gon' do nothing crazy, is he?"

"Naw, but I better go make sure."

Keyla, Treyvon, and Rashawn were outside in front of the hotel. By the time we made it to the door, Keyla and Rashawn were coming in, arguing back and forth.

"I don't know why you invited the nigga here in the first place. You knew you was gon' give me the pussy."

"Fuck you, Shawn. I planned on staying as far away from you as possible because you ain't for nothing real."

"Man, why we gotta put labels on the shit? Let's just go with the flow."

I wasn't sure how long they went back and forth like that, but Rashaad and I went straight to the dance floor and danced the night away.

22

RASHAAD

The week following our trip to Atlanta was busy as hell. We were having a seventies-themed party at the rink for Rashawn's thirty-fourth birthday that weekend, and although we'd been planning since the grand opening, there were still some minor details we had to take care of.

At the same time, Aubrielle was busy ensuring that all of her students were ready for the upcoming fall festival, which was two weeks away. Not only was she the choreographer for Zara's class, but she also had three other classes. With everything that we had going on, we hadn't seen each other all week except on FaceTime.

Another reason we hadn't connected in person was because she was still refusing to stay the night at my house. I understood and appreciated her reasons, but she was gon' have to get over it. I planned to have a conversation with Zara to make sure that she knew how I felt about Aubrielle and that she was the woman I planned to build a future with. I hoped her little six-year-old brain understood.

It was Thursday evening, and I'd just picked Zara up from my parents' house. Thankfully, she was fed and had done most of her homework. Once we finished the rest of it, she took a bath, and I let her watch TV while I showered. I was surprised but glad that she was still awake when I was finished.

"Hey, Zee. Daddy wants to talk to you about something serious."

"Okay, Daddy. Is it good serious or bad serious?"

I sat in the recliner and motioned for her to come sit on my lap.

"I think it's a good serious."

"Okay, well, let's hear it."

This girl!

"Do you remember when Daddy went out of town with Ms. Aubrielle and uncle Shawn?"

"Yes."

"Do you remember when you called me, and you wanted to talk to Ms. Aubrielle, but I told you she was busy?"

"No, you said she was running errands, but I knew she wasn't, because I could see her in the window."

"I know, Miss Smarty-Pants. Do you remember what you told me to tell Ms. Aubrielle before we got off the phone?"

"Daddy, I have a great memory. I remember everything."

"What did you say?"

"I said for you to tell her that I loved her."

"Did you mean it?"

"You told me not to say things that I don't mean, Daddy. I do love Ms. Aubrielle. In class, she's always very nice to me and the other kids, even if we don't get something right, and when she goes places with me and you, we have a lot of fun. I wish she was my mommy."

Shit! I wasn't prepared for that.

"You, umm, you do?"

"Ummhmm, because I can tell she likes you a whole lot, and you like her a lot, too."

"I do."

"Do you love her?"

This damn girl!

"I do love her, Zee. But listen, I don't want you to feel like Ms. Aubrielle is here to replace your mother. I know her leaving is hard for you to understand. I'm a grown-up, and I don't understand it.

Your mother and I were good friends, and if it weren't for her, I wouldn't have you. Do you understand that?"

"Yes, Daddy. You told me that before."

"Ms. Aubrielle and I are more than good friends, and I love her like how Pop-Pop loves Gigi."

She giggled and said, "That's a whole lot, Daddy."

"It is. There may be some times when she spends the night here with us. You think you'd be cool with that?"

"Yes. If you marry her, she would live with us and be here all the time."

Really, Zee?

"I'd like to marry her one day. You think if I asked her, she'd say yes?"

"She will if she loves you like Gigi loves Pop-Pop."

What the hell am I gonna do with this little girl?

BY THE TIME Saturday night rolled around, I was irritable, horny, and dare I say... excited. It was the night of Rashawn's party, and Aubrielle was meeting at the rink. I didn't care what was going on when she got there, we were going directly to my office, and I would be bending her ass over the back of my chair.

"This shit is dope!" Rashawn said.

We'd just finished our last walk-through before opening the doors. Rasheeda came up with the décor concept and did a great job. I definitely felt like I was in a time warp.

"It is, so don't complain when you see the bill," Rasheeda told him.

"Is our surprise celebrity MC here?" I asked.

We had multiple contests and games planned for the night and had booked one of the most well-known voices of D.C. radio to emcee the event. When we met with him last month, he seemed more excited about the event than we were.

"Yeah, he's over there talking to the DJ. I still can't believe we got Donnie Simpson to emcee tonight," Rashaad said.

"What I can't believe is how fine that man still is. If he wasn't old enough to be my father, I'd be trying to call him daddy," Rasheeda said, divulging way more information that we wanted to hear, causing me and Rashawn to walk away.

We gave Barry the signal to open the doors. The DJ had already started spinning hits from tonight's chosen decade. In no time, the floor was filled with people dressed in their seventies' best, having the time of their lives. With all three of us here, along with ninety-five percent of our staff, I expected things to run smoothly.

I tried to keep myself occupied, but I couldn't stop myself from glancing at the door every few minutes, hoping to see Aubrielle. Just when I was about to go to my office and call her, my eyes caught a glimpse of my beautiful ray of light.

With her skates thrown across her shoulder and a hand on her hip, she scanned the area. When they landed on me, she smiled but didn't move in my direction. I guess she expected me to come to her, which I had no problem doing because she was closer to my office. As I made my way to her, maneuvering around the people blocking my path, I made note of her appearance.

Aubrielle had her hair slicked back away from her face, and on the top of her head was a huge Afro puff. The hot-pink crop top she was wearing was tight and stopped right underneath her breasts. My eyes continued to travel down to the matching old-school running shorts, causing my dick brick up. I hadn't seen her from behind yet, but I was positive her ass cheeks were exposed. Around her waist sat a silver fanny pack, and she finished off her look with a pair of white knee-socks with pink stripes. On her feet were a pair of running shoes.

"Damn, I missed you," I said when I reached her, before kissing her lips.

"I missed you, too."

"Let's go to my office. There's something important I need to give you."

Taking her by the hand, we went to my office, and I made sure I locked the door behind me.

"You look good, Elle. Take all that shit off."

Without hesitating, she toed off her shoes, kicking them out of the way, lifted her shirt over her head, unsnapped the fanny pack, and shimmied out of her shorts, tossing everything to the side. My brain was telling me that I should be pissed off at the fact that she wasn't wearing panties or a bra, but my dick was excited as hell.

She stood there, butt ass naked, except for the knee-socks, with all of her weight on one leg and her hand on her hip, waiting for me to tell her what to do next or make a move.

"Turn around. Put your hands on my desk. Spread your legs. Toot that ass up."

I waited until she completed each command before I gave another. She was positioned perfectly for me to slide right up in her. Whipping my dick out, I stroked it as I admired the view.

"You came ready for me, huh?"

"Ye—Ah, shit!"

I pushed inside of her before she could fully answer me. Her pussy sucked me in, and she immediately started throwing that ass back. I tightened my grip on either side of her waist to gain some control. If I let her continue at the pace she was going, this wouldn't last long.

"Damn, Elle. You really missed a nigga."

"Ummhmm."

"Slow down, baby. This dick ain't going nowhere."

Keeping one hand on her waist, I used the other to reach around to her pussy. When I found her clit, I massaged it at the same tempo that my dick slid in and out of her gushiness.

"Shit, baby!" Elle damn near shouted.

The first time we were intimate in my office, she was worried about people hearing her. She didn't give a damn about that now.

My hand moved to her back, and I pressed, pushing her chest against my desk, changing my angle of entry. It must have felt good to her because she began moaning and warning me of her pending orgasm. The moment she started to cum, her pussy tightened around my dick. I wanted to hold on a little longer, but it felt too good. She milked my nut right on outta me, and I filled her with my seeds.

As my nut sack emptied, I laid on top of her, and we remained that way well after the throbbing of our genitals had stopped. It was quite possible that I'd fallen asleep. I opened my eyes when I heard her called my name.

"Rashaad, get up."

"Hmm?"

"Baby, you're heavy. Get up."

Once we were disconnected from each other, I backed away to give her some room. I had to look away because my dick wanted some more action. I'd have her in here all night if there weren't a party going on, on the other side of my office door.

When she finally stood, she grabbed her things from where she tossed them and went back to my desk. She removed from inside her fanny pack a pair of thongs, a bra, and a pack of wipes. After taking some wipes out of the package, she handed them to me. I was still standing with my pants down and my dick semi-hard, glistening with the combination of our fluids.

"You came prepared, I see, and don't think I didn't peep that your ass didn't have on no panties or bra."

"You didn't like that?"

"I loved it. A whole bunch of other niggas probably loved it, too. Did you wear a jacket or something?"

"But all they can do is look because what I got is only for you. It's not that cold out, so I left my jacket in the car."

She took a few steps toward me and stood on her toes to kiss me.

"I knew you'd have me in your office at some point tonight. I had to make sure I had something to clean myself up with so your children wouldn't be dripping down my legs all day night."

23

AUBRIELLE

The party vibe had gone up another level by the time Rashaad and I made it back out there. I was upset that I'd missed the Limbo on Skates competition because I wanted to participate. Donnie Simpson had just awarded the winners, and I had to beg Rashaad to take me to meet him. When he finally agreed, I was giddy as hell, and I think that made him a little jealous. *Oh well!* Donnie was a legend, and there was no way I would be in the same space as him and not meet him.

After I'd taken all the pictures I could take, had him sign my fanny pack, and FaceTimed my mom, Rashaad finally dragged me away.

"I need to get some of these pictures printed out so I can frame them," I said as I excitedly swiped through the pics we'd taken.

"And put them where?" Rashaad asked.

"I don't know. On my dresser, the nightstand, maybe on the wall."

"Elle, if I come to your house and see framed pictures of another nigga, we gon' have a problem."

"But it's Donnie Simpson."

"I don't care if it's Barack Obama. Stop playing with me."

His jealousy was cute, and I couldn't stop laughing at him.

"When Keyla gets here, you'll have to take us back over so she can meet him, too."

"Naw, I'm not doing that. Shawn can take her if she wants to meet him," he told me, shaking his head.

"You know they're barely speaking to each other. She didn't even want to come tonight, but she promised me she'd come for a little bit when she got off work. She should be here soon."

"If she wants to meet Donnie, she better make up with Shawn," he said.

I felt my phone vibrate in my hand and looked down at it.

"Oh, Keyla's here. I'm gonna go find her."

I kissed his cheek and skated to where Keyla said she was waiting. When I spotted her, she was talking to none other than Treyvon. They looked to be having a serious conversation, but I was about to interrupt all that.

"Hey, Key. I thought you might have changed your mind. Hey, Treyvon. It's good to see you again."

"You, too. I'll let you ladies enjoy your night. Keyla, I'll talk to you soon."

We both watched him skate over to a couple of guys and strike up a conversation. When I looked at Keyla, right away, she was in defense mode.

"It was just a coincidence. I did not invite him here."

"I didn't say a word."

"Yeah, but you were looking at me like I did something wrong."

"Naw, cousin. That's that guilt. You need to gon' head and tell Treyvon that Rashawn has the best dick you ever had and right now, you're not ready to move on from that. But anyway, you look cute."

Keyla was wearing a pair of high-waisted bell-bottom jeans and a shimmery bra as her top. Her hair was in a high ponytail that hung down to her waist.

"Thank you! You do, too. What did Rashaad have to say about your outfit?"

"Ha! Nothing. He just took me in his office and gave me something long and strong."

"I swear to God. I'm never going in his office. Y'all stay in there fucking."

We heard the voice of Donnie Simpson encouraging all the ladies onto the floor for a ladies' only skate. As we headed that way, I excitedly told Keyla about meeting him, promising to show her the pictures later. When the music to "Ladies Night" by Kool & The Gang started, all the ladies cheered. Those that could skate well did their thing as they skated around the outer perimeter. Keyla and I were in that group, and although we didn't have a routine to that song, we knew each other well enough to be in sync. Right after that, "I'm Every Woman" by Chaka Khan blasted through the speakers, soliciting another round of cheers, and literally, every woman in there was on the skate floor.

I spent the rest of the night with Keyla while Rashaad worked. He checked in with me every so often to make sure we didn't need anything. Rasheeda skated with us for a little while, lusting over Donnie Simpson every time we passed him. Apparently, he wasn't Keyla's type, so she didn't understand our excitement. Something had to be wrong with her because only a blind, crazy woman wouldn't find him attractive.

After midnight, Keyla decided it was time for her to head home because she had to work in the morning. So far, she had steered clear of Rashawn, but her luck ran out as we walked toward the exit.

"Damn! You gon' leave without telling your boy happy birthday?" Rashawn snuck up on her from behind and put his arms around her. I could tell from his demeanor that he was a little tipsy.

Keyla wiggled out of his arms and turned to face him before saying, "Happy birthday, Shawn. I hope you're enjoying your party."

"The party is cool, but I know something I'd like even better."

He reached for her waist, put his index fingers through her belt loops, and then pulled her body against his. When he leaned down to try to kiss her, she turned her head and pushed him away.

"I told you I'm not doing this with you. Have a good night."

Without saying goodbye to me, she was gone. Rashawn watched her leave with an angry expression on his face.

"Your cousin needs to stop tripping," he told me.

"Oh, she's tripping because she's not accepting any old thing from you? Miss me with all that nonsense."

I skated away from him before he could reply. I had no idea where Rashaad was, so I found a spot on the wall and watched the couples' skate competition that was currently taking place. If Rashaad and I were able to compete, we would've embarrassed these folks.

About twenty minutes had passed, and I still hadn't seen my man. When I pulled out my phone to text him, a woman leaned against the wall, standing unnecessarily close to me. I took a step to the side and finished my text to Rashaad.

"You're pretty," the woman said.

"Thank you."

"I love your outfit."

"Thank you, again. Yours is nice, too."

A text from Rashaad came through, telling me to give him about ten minutes.

"Are you and Rashaad serious?" she asked.

I was sure the expression on my face was one of annoyance and surprise. I didn't know this lady from Adam, and she was trying to be all up in my business.

"Excuse me?"

"Rashaad... You're dating him, right?"

"Why is that your business?"

"I've seen you with him a few times and was just wondering. He doesn't do serious relationships."

"Who the fuck are you, and why do you feel the need to share your thoughts with me?"

"I'm Joanna. Rashaad and used to... Well, we kind of had a thing. Nothing serious, though, because he doesn't do serious relationships."

"Oh really?"

"I'm just here to warn you. I don't want you to waste your time thinking what you're doing with him is anything more than a fling. You'll never meet his parents, and he probably didn't even mention to you that he has a daughter."

"Look, I'm sorry that—actually, I'm not sorry. You can—"

"My bad, baby. I—Joanna? You two know each other?" Rashaad asked with a look of confusion.

"No, baby. She felt the need to introduce herself to me and warn me not to waste my time with you, because you don't do serious relationships," I told him.

"Joanna, if you don't take your ass on some got damn where. The fuck kinda shit you on?"

"I was simply telling her the truth," she defended.

"No, you told her your truth. You lucky my mama raised me to respect women. There's a few choice words I'd have for your ass. Let's go, Elle." Like that whole incident hadn't just occurred, he said, "You coming home with me, right?"

"So you gon' just act like Joanna didn't just approach me on some bullshit."

"Fuck Joanna's ass. Don't give whatever she said any energy. You coming home with me?"

I decided not to make a big deal out it since it was clear that she was one of his old fuck-buddies.

"Since Zara is with her grandparents, I think I can do that."

"I told you I talked to her, and she's cool with you staying the night."

"And I told you I'd give it some thought. Are you staying until closing?"

"Unfortunately, I am. Since it's Shawn's birthday, Sheeda and I agreed to close. He probably found somebody to go home with already."

"He tried to act like he wanted Key to be that person, but she dismissed his ass. He had a whole attitude about it, too."

"They'll figure it out. There's still another hour before closing. I'll give you the keys to my office, and you can chill in there until it's time to go."

"Naw, I'm good out here. I'll just watch Donnie Simpson until you're ready. I should go see if he needs some help."

"Ha, ha! You ain't funny, Elle. Here are my keys in case you chase your mind."

After handing me his keys, he grabbed my ass cheeks and pulled me to his chest before kissing my forehead and disappearing into the crowd.

24

RASHAAD

By the time Aubrielle, Rasheeda, and I walked out of the rink, the temperature had dropped quite a bit. I'd given Aubrielle my jacket, but it only covered just past her ass, leaving her legs completely exposed. I had to make sure my sister made it to her car safely before I walked Aubrielle to hers, so she was shivering by the time we headed in that direction.

"Shaad!" I heard from a voice that sounded eerily like Carmen.

Aubrielle and I stopped walking and turned in the direction of the voice.

"What the fuck are you doing here?" I asked Carmen.

"I didn't know your address, so coming here was the only other way to find you unless I went to your parents' house."

"What do you want?"

"I, umm, I need to give you something, but it's in the car. Can you, umm, walk with me?"

"Carmen, I ain't got time for no bullshit. What's so important that you need to give it to me in the middle of the damn night?"

"Please, Shaad. I wouldn't be here if it wasn't important."

I could feel Aubrielle shivering, which reminded me that I needed to get her to her car. I looked at her but couldn't read her expression.

"Where are you parked? I need to make sure she gets to her car—"

"No, I'm good. Let's go see what she has that's so important."

I thought I detected an attitude in Aubrielle's voice, and I could understand if she had one. We were several feet behind Carmen as we followed her to her car.

"What do you think it is?" Aubrielle asked.

"I have no idea. I haven't communicated with her since she left."

The longer we walked, the more my mind raced. Not knowing what to expect had me a little nervous. Carmen reached the car before we did and stood by the driver's side rear door. We were cautious as we neared her, standing a few feet away.

"Look, Shaad. When I found out about this, it was too late for me to do anything about it."

"Carmen, stop beating around the bush and tell me why you're here."

She pulled the door open and stepped to the side. Because it was dark, I had to get closer to make sure my eyes weren't deceiving me. I was speechless when I confirmed what I saw. Taking a step back, I looked at Carmen.

"Who's baby is that?"

"Ours."

"The fuck you mean *ours*?"

Without saying another word, Carmen popped the trunk and pulled out a large suitcase.

"Here are his things. He's six weeks old and a good baby. I tried, Shaad. I tried to do the right thing, but I don't have it in me to be a mother. I thought about putting him up for adoption, but I know he's yours, and I didn't think that'd be fair."

While she spoke, she took the baby out of the car, along with a diaper bag, put them both on the ground next to my feet, and then covered the car seat with a blanket.

"We can meet next week, and I'll sign over my rights. My number is still the same. I'm sorry you had to find out like this, but there was no other way."

I was speechless as I tried to process what was happening. *This had to be a nightmare.* Before I could get my thoughts together enough to ask the questions that needed to be asked, Carmen had hopped in her car and was gone.

I looked at the car seat that sat on the ground next to me, then at the diaper bag and suitcase, before slowly bringing my eyes up to meet Aubrielle's.

"You lied to me," she whispered.

"Baby, I—"

"The fact that you let her leave him here means that there is a possibility that he's yours. You lied to me when you didn't have to."

She took my jacket off and tossed it on top of the suitcase.

"If I can't trust you to be honest about your past, how can I trust you with my future? I knew you were too good to be true."

Before I could respond, she ran in the opposite direction. I shouted her name repeatedly, but she didn't stop or turn around. Off in the distance, I heard a car start and seconds later, screeching tires. I didn't move until I heard cries underneath the blanket.

"What the fuck just happened?"

WHEN I MADE IT HOME, I unloaded the baby and his belongings, then went inside. He'd been quiet since his crying spell in the parking lot of RBL after I gave him the pacifier that was clipped to his shirt. In my bedroom, I lifted his sleeping body out of the car seat and laid him on the bed.

His skin tone was the same as mine and even with his eyes closed, he looked a lot like Zara. The texture of his hair was soft and curly, but he was young, so I knew that could change. I had a million thoughts going through my head, but the main one plaguing my mind was, *how the fuck did I let this happen?*

"I don't even know your name, lil' man."

My voice startled him a little, and he stretched his chunky body out but didn't wake up. Picking up his diaper bag, I dug through it, finding the usual things, but his birth certificate was in one of the side pockets.

"Rashaad Khalil Hanes, Jr., born on September seventh, at 8:09 a.m. Eight pounds, six ounces, and twenty-three inches long."

I looked at him as he made baby noises in his sleep and replayed the scene in the parking lot. Carmen said that it was too late to do anything about it when she found out about this. That means that she was pregnant before she left and didn't know. I wasn't a woman and didn't claim to know everything there was to know about their anatomy, but a woman not knowing that she was pregnant, especially after a few months, baffled me.

It was close to four in the morning, and I was still trying to process all that had transpired. If my uncle Abe were alive, he'd be here giving me a hard time, but afterward, he'd follow it up with some sound advice. I knew I couldn't call my parents at this time of night with this kind of information. It would throw them into a full panic. I grabbed my phone and called my only other alternatives.

"Oh my God, Shaad! This better be important," my sister said when she picked up.

"It is. I need you at my house ASAP."

"What? You want me to get up?"

"Sheeda, please. I swear if this wasn't important, I wouldn't be calling."

Releasing a deep sigh, she agreed and hung up. Next, I called Rashawn. When he didn't answer, I kept calling until he did.

"Nigga, what the fuck?" he answered.

"Bruh, I need you to come to my house… *now.*"

"You've got to be fucking kidding me. What time is it?"

"It don't matter. Just get here."

I ended the call and tossed my phone on the bed. When I glanced at Rashaad Jr., his eyes were open, and he was looking at me. We had a stare down for a good twenty seconds, and suddenly, he smiled. My heart turned to mush, and I picked him up, cradling him in my arms.

"You're the most unexpected surprise, but I love you already, lil' man. I can't wait to introduce you to your sister. Then we'll all have to put our heads together and figure out how to get my Elle back."

He cooed in response to my rambling.

"You think she'll take me back? No? I know I wasn't completely honest, but once I explain it to her, she'll understand."

He cooed some more and began squirming in my arms.

"Elle is an amazing woman, son. I think you'll like her. Your sister loves her."

He continued to squirm, and his coos turned into whining. I placed him on the bed to check his diaper, and he needed to be changed. After taking care of that, I fed him one of the bottles I found in his bag. He guzzled it down in no time and burped within seconds of me putting him on my shoulder. I thought changing him and feeding him would put him back to sleep, but he was extremely alert and ready to kick it.

"I guess it's cool if you stay up to meet your aunt and uncle."

I put him in his car seat, and we went to my family room to wait for my siblings. Rashaad Jr. was content on the floor next to the recliner, sucking on his fist. I began to doze off when someone rang the doorbell. Before I got to the door, Rasheeda was letting herself in, and Rashawn was behind her.

"This must be serious if you called us both here. Ma and Dad coming, too?"

"No. I'm not ready for them to know this yet. Follow me."

In the family room, the car seat was positioned on the side of the recliner that they couldn't see. When I lifted him out of the car seat, their reaction was what I expected.

"What the fuck?" came from Rashawn.

"Who's baby is that?" came from Rasheeda.

"Meet your nephew, Rashaad Jr."

"Bruh!"

"Are you serious?"

"I think y'all should have a seat," I told them.

I sat in the recliner with my son in my arms and told them what happened in the parking lot of RBL. It wasn't a long story, but they both were looking as if I'd left something out.

"You and Carmen were still fucking?" Rashawn asked.

"Seriously, Shaad, I thought you stop dealing with her like that years ago. What the hell happened?" Rasheeda added.

Taking a deep breath, I told them about a night that I'd been trying hard to forget.

"As y'all know, when Uncle Abe died, I probably took it the hardest. One night, my head was all fucked up about it, and I was drinking. By the time Carmen came home, I was tore up. She tried to console me, and we ended up having sex. The next day, she was naked in my bed, and I didn't know why, because I had no recollection of what happened. When she told me we had sex, she couldn't understand why I was pissed, claiming I wanted to as much as she did. All I wanted to do was forget it happened."

"That bitch! She knew you were vulnerable and drunk. I swear to God I can't stand her," Rasheeda vented.

"Are you sure he's yours? Does the timing match up?" Rashawn questioned.

"It does, but I still plan to get a DNA test."

"Let me hold him."

Rasheeda came and took Rashaad Jr. out of my arms.

"Damn, Shaad. No test needed. He looks just like Zara, who looks just like you. Hey, nephew."

"I don't give a damn who he looks like, get a test. Carmen is not to be trusted," Rashawn said.

"I am, but I think he's mine."

"This explains why Aubrielle came home, unexpectedly, and pissed off," Rashawn said. "She almost caught me and Key in a very compromising position, but she was so mad she didn't even notice us."

"She left me in the parking lot, in the middle of the night, with a damn baby."

"Damn, that's kinda cold," Rasheeda commented between the kisses she was leaving all over my son's cheeks.

"I can understand her being upset, but it's not like you cheated on her. You didn't even know her when he was conceived."

"I don't think she's mad about him, per se. She feels like I lied to her."

"About?" he asked.

"I told her that Carmen and I hadn't been involved romantically since Zee was a year old."

"And, like most would, she assumed that it meant y'all weren't fucking, right?" Rasheeda guessed.

"We weren't."

"All it takes is one time. Let me hold him," Rashawn said to Rasheeda, then took Rashaad Jr. out of her arms. "Wassup, nephew. Your daddy is a damn fool."

"Don't be telling him shit like that, Shawn."

"It's true, though," my sister agreed. "How you gon' fix things with Aubrielle?"

"I don't know, but I'll fix it. I can't lie, though. I'm kinda pissed that she left like that. She ain't give me a chance to explain at all."

"Sorry, big bro. I'm with Aubrielle. If I'd been thinking my nigga ain't had sex with his baby mama in five or six years, and his baby mama showed up with an infant that she says is his, I ain't trying to hear a word the nigga gotta say."

"But—"

"Ain't no buts, bro. Put yourself in her shoes. You may not have outright lied to her, but you omitted a significant part of the truth. You think if she'd known all the details that she would've still left?"

"Probably not."

"Exactly. Now, it's damn near daybreak, and I'm tired as hell. Somebody needs to get enough sleep to manage the rink tomorrow, and that clearly won't be you, and Shawn has the day off. I'm going home."

"That's how you feel?"

"That's exactly how I feel. Let me know what I can do to help, and good luck telling Ma and Dad."

Rasheeda kissed Rashawn's cheek, then did some baby talk to her nephew before kissing his cheek as well. I got up to walk her to the door.

"Congratulations, Shaad. I know this ain't the most ideal situation, but babies are a blessing. Give Aubrielle some time to cool off and then be honest with her. I can see how much she loves you, and I'm sure it hurt her to think that you lied to her."

She gave me a hug and a kiss on the cheek before leaving. I watched her until she was safely in her car and pulling off. Back in the family room, Rashaad Jr. had fallen asleep in his uncle's arms.

"He seems to be a pretty chill baby. Granted, it's six a.m., but he hasn't cried since I've been here."

"Yeah, Carmen said he's a good baby."

"Bruh, how did you keep yourself from choking her out?"

"Besides the fact that I don't put my hands on women like that, I was in shock. Shit, I'm still in shock."

"As you should be. I could be knee-deep in Keyla's pussy had you not called, but this was definitely an emergency. I'm about to head out, though."

He stood with my son in his arms and brought him over to me. As I was about to stand, he said, "Naw, stay put. I'll lock up."

I was already reclined in the chair, so I took Rashaad Jr. and positioned him on my chest, then tossed the blanket that was on the arm of the chair over us. I was probably asleep before Rashawn was in his car.

25

AUBRIELLE

When I woke up, my eyes felt swollen. I could only imagine what I looked like after crying for hours before falling asleep. The fact that I woke up in my bed confirmed that what happened last night, or early this morning, was not a dream. I reached for my phone on the nightstand and didn't see a single missed call from Rashaad. Although I was pissed off at him, that had me in my feelings a little.

"This nigga didn't even attempt to call me. Wow!"

It was only eight a.m., and any other time, I would have rolled over and gone back to sleep. My bladder was about to explode, and as much as I wanted to bury myself under my comforter, I got up to use the bathroom. After relieving my bladder, I opened the door to find Keyla standing against the wall with her arms folded across her chest.

"You look like shit. Tell me what happened," she demanded.

"What makes you think something happened?"

"Oh, maybe the fact that you walked in on Rashawn eating my pussy on the kitchen counter—don't worry, it's been completely sanitized—and didn't even notice us. Oh, and don't let me forget that Rashaad called Rashawn at four in the morning, telling him to get to his place ASAP."

"Eww. You have a whole bedroom, and y'all were on the kitchen counter? Wait! Are y'all back together?"

"I mean, he was eating in the kitchen, and we would have had to be together in the first place to be *back* together. But don't try to change the subject. Something happened, and my gut is telling me it's serious. I have ten minutes before I need to leave for work. Get to talking."

Walking past her into my bedroom, I tried to close the door in her face, but I wasn't quick enough.

"Bri, stop playing."

"Okay, fine! He told me he hadn't fucked his baby mama since Zara was one. Well, the baby that she dropped off in the parking lot of the skating rink proves that, *that* was a lie!"

"Wait, I'm confused. Are you saying that Rashaad's baby mama dropped a baby off in the parking lot?" I nodded. "And this baby supposedly belongs to him?" I nodded again. "What did he do?"

"Nothing."

"What do you mean nothing? He—"

"I mean, once she told him it was *their* baby, he did and said nothing. She took the baby and all of his belongings out of the car and took off like she was never there."

"Damn!"

"When I accused him of lying to me, he didn't deny it. When I walked—well, jogged away—he didn't come after me, and I don't have one missed call from him. All that tells me is that he's guilty."

"If he had denied lying, would you have believed him?"

"No."

"If he had come after you, would you have listened to him?"

"No."

"If he had called you, would you have answered?"

"Hell no!"

"Why are you upset if you weren't going to hear him out or believe what he had to say?"

"Because… because… because he's in the wrong, and he should be begging me for my forgiveness."

"Bri, he found out he was the father of a newborn son just a few hours ago, and that newborn was left in his care. As much as he may want to explain his side and get your forgiveness, he's probably a little busy. I'm on your side, cousin. If he was still sleeping with his baby mama, he didn't have a reason to lie about it. It makes him seem untrustworthy, but maybe he thought lying was necessary."

"Whatever!" I said, knowing she was right. Crawling into my bed, I pulled the comforter over my head.

"Whatever my ass. Hiding under that blanket ain't gon' change nothing. I understand why you're mad, and you have the right to be, but you love that man, like for real, for real. So what? He didn't tell the whole truth about his relationship with his ex. Anything that went down between them happened before you. It's not like he cheated on you."

Tossing the comforter off my head and sitting up, I said, "But he lied for no reason, and if he lied about that, who knows what else he's hiding."

"Like I said, I'm sure he had his reasons. Look, I gotta go, but think about the number of times you forgave Damon for his bullshit and you had the proof slapping you in the face."

With that, Keyla was gone, leaving me to wallow in sadness alone. I felt around the bed for my phone. As my hand landed on it, it vibrated and startled me. Part of me wanted it to be Rashaad, even though I had no intention of communicating with him. However, it was only Keyla.

Key: You don't have to wait for him to reach out to you. You did walk out on him.

I didn't bother to reply to her. She was crazy if she thought I should contact him when he was the one who lied. I fell back on my mountain of pillows and went to my Instagram page. Even though I wasn't huge on social media, I had over ten thousand followers. My personal posts were very minimal, but I did post a lot of videos of me dancing to help promote my dance classes.

Of course, I went to Rashaad's page to see if he had posted anything. At first, it didn't look like he had, but once the page refreshed, there it was. He'd secretly taken some pictures of me and

Zara while I was reading her a bedtime story. The caption read: *My favorite ladies.* My heart skipped a beat when I saw that he'd just posted it thirty minutes ago.

"Lord, why'd he have to lie, though?"

I must have fallen back to sleep, because my ringing and vibrating phone startled me awake. Squinting at the screen, I saw that it was my mom, and although I didn't feel like talking, I went ahead and answered it.

"Hey, Ma."

"Hey, Bri. You still sleep?"

"I was up earlier but must have dozed off again. I'm glad you guys made it back from your cruise safely. How was it?"

"Oh, Bri! It was amazing," she said with excitement. I could hear the smile in her voice. "You and Rashaad have to go on one for your honeymoon."

Just hearing his name almost made me break down. I guess my mother was expecting some sort of response, and when she didn't get one, she picked up on my mood.

"What's wrong? Did something happen between you and Rashaad?"

"I don't want to talk about it, Ma."

"Why not? You've never kept anything from us regarding your relationships. Every time you found out that fool Damon cheated on you, you came right to me and your father. We've always prided ourselves on letting you live your life and letting you learn from any mistakes you make. Now, I like you and Rashaad together. I hope whatever is going on, it's not too serious."

I took a minute to think about whether or not I wanted to share before spilling my guts to her. I didn't know that while I was telling her what happened, my father had walked into the room, and she put me on speaker. When I heard his voice, I groaned inwardly.

"You mean to tell me that nigga got another baby? Is it with the same baby mama that he said he wasn't sleeping with?" my dad asked.

I could tell by the tone of his voice that he was pissed. He sounded the same way he did when I would tell them about Damon's indiscretions. I always had to beg my dad not to do him bodily harm, and he was able to refrain, except that one time.

It was after I'd spent the night crying at their house about Damon's cheating. My dad left our house on a mission to find him and set him straight. He went to Damon's house, where I was living, and ended up roughing him up pretty badly. The only reason Damon didn't press charges was because I promised not to leave him. My dad didn't talk to me for a month, and once he did, he stopped being a part of any conversation about Damon.

"Technically, he never said he wasn't sleeping with her. He said they weren't—"

"Romantically involved," he said, finishing my sentence. "I know what he said, and I don't need you defending another no-good nigga. Obviously, you got a problem with it, or you wouldn't be on this phone sounded like somebody died!"

"But Daddy—"

"Don't *but Daddy* me. It's like we didn't set a good example, and you keep falling in love with the same bum ass niggas over and over again."

"Him not telling me the whole truth doesn't make him a bum, Daddy, and I'm not gonna let you talk about him like that. *Yes*, I'm upset, but Rashaad is nothing like Damon or any other man that I've ever dated, and I won't let you put him in that category."

"Aubrey, your daughter has lost her damn mind. Let me leave this conversation before I book a flight and come remind you who the hell you talking to, lil' girl."

His voice got faint, and I assumed he was walking away.

"Ma, why didn't you tell me Daddy was listening?"

"Because I didn't think it was a problem. It never has been before."

"Yeah, but he already had some reservations about Rashaad, even though I thought everything was cool by the time we left Atlanta."

"Bri, your dad has never liked any man you've gotten serious about. Rashaad was the first that he seemed to warm up to."

"Well, that's been ruined."

"Look, sweetheart. Regardless of how your father and I feel, you need to decide how you want to move forward. Before you make any final decisions, though, talk to the man. Something is telling me that there is more to this story."

"I'm sure I will eventually, Ma. All of this just happened, so I need some time to sort out my feelings."

"Take as much time as you need. I'll talk to you Wednesday, but if you need to talk before then, call me."

"Okay. I love you, and can you talk to your husband and tell him he's wrong about Rashaad?"

"I'll talk to him. Love you, too."

MONDAY EVENING HAD ARRIVED, and I was nervous about the possibility of seeing Rashaad. I wasn't sure he would be bringing Zara to dance class, but a small part of hoped that he would. *Who am I fooling? A big part of me did.* This morning, I was greeted by an *I love you* text from him that made me put my phone against my heart and whisper, "I love you, too," as I held back tears. I didn't reply to the text, and unfortunately, I didn't hear from him again.

As I prepped for her class, I heard the door open, and Zara came barreling in. When she reached me, she wrapped her arms around my waist, and in true Zara form, she hit me with, "Ms. Aubrielle, did you see my baby brother?"

"Hey, sweetheart. No, I didn't see him. I'm sure he's adorable."

"He is. My daddy is taking care of him, so Titi brought me to class."

I looked toward the door, and Rasheeda stood there with her hands in the front pocket of her hoodie.

"Okay. Maybe I'll see him soon. Go get ready for class."

As usual, she skipped away, doing what she was told, while I went over to talk to Rasheeda.

"Hey," I said casually.

"How are you?" she asked.

"I'm good."

We stood there quietly for an uncomfortable amount of seconds before she spoke again.

"I'm sure you're wondering—"

"I'm not. I'm good."

"Girl, go lie to somebody else. Shaad hasn't called you yet because I told him to give you some space. I know if I were you, I'd need a minute to process. He's dealing with a lot, so I'm not sure when he'll call, but when does, pick up the phone."

"Did he tell you how he lied to me?"

"He told me, and now that I know everything, I wouldn't say he lied, but he didn't tell the whole truth. Listen, Shaad is my brother, so I'm gon' ride for him regardless... him and Shawn. But men do stupid shit for no reason. I mean, for absolutely no reason they do dumb shit. However, that doesn't mean I won't tell their asses when they're wrong, and Shaad was wrong. Can you do me a favor?"

I shrugged my shoulders, then said, "Sure."

"Don't make any decisions about your relationship until you hear him out. He's messed up about all this, but he knows he has no one to blame but himself."

Not waiting for me to reply, she pulled the door open and went to the seating area. I remained standing next to the door, thinking about what she, as well as my mother and Keyla, said. *Hear him out.* A few more kids trickled in, and soon, we began the final preparations for the fall festival. It was a welcomed distraction and helped me make it through the rest of the evening.

26

RASHAAD

*M*y parents' reaction when I told them they had a grandson was exactly what I expected. Once my parents got over the shock and confusion, they let me explain how he came to be and how he ended up with me. My mother was so pissed that she forgot Zara was there for a minute and called Carmen everything but a child of God. My father was speechless. They'd never been fond of Carmen, and this situation only gave them more reason not to like her.

Zara didn't understand how she came to have a baby brother, but she was excited about it and didn't much care. I had a feeling that some extra therapy sessions would be needed once the excitement wore off and she was able to process what was going on. I would definitely be sitting in on those sessions for my own healing.

After my parents loved on R.J., they asked how Aubrielle felt about everything. When I told them her reaction, they weren't surprised, but they encouraged me to talk to her and make things right. That was a week ago, and I still hadn't reached out to her. I missed her like crazy, too.

Zara and I had been staying with my parents for the past week. Just the few hours I had alone with my son the night I brought him home was enough to let me know I needed help. Thank God my parents didn't mind stepping in until I got the hang of having a newborn again, along with a precocious six-year-old.

Today was the day of the fall festival, and even if we didn't get a chance to talk, I knew I'd see Aubrielle. Every morning and night this week, I sent her text telling her that I loved and missed her. She never replied, but I honestly wasn't expecting her to. Each day, I thought about going to see her, but something in my spirit told me it wasn't time. The one time I didn't listen to my spirit, Carmen happened, so I was obedient and stayed away. However, today couldn't be avoided. Zara had no idea what was going on between us, and I hoped it would be resolved before she realized there was a problem.

My whole family was front and center in the auditorium. Keyla had even come along to support, and we filled up half of the row. The lights dimmed, and the crowd settled down. My mother was holding Rashaad Jr., and he seemed to be content. Zara's class would be the first to go, and I was excited to see how everything they'd been practicing would come together.

When the beat dropped to "Toast" by the Jamaican artist Koffee, I knew we were in for a fantastic show. All of the dance studios were soundproof, so I had no idea what they'd be dancing to, even though I attended most of Zara's lessons. The curtains opened, and my baby girl was front and center, but right away, I could tell something was off. I could see it in her eyes and the expression on her face. When I dropped her off a couple of hours earlier, she was fine, so I said a little prayer that it was only my imagination.

Everyone else began the routine, and Zara was frozen in place. About a minute passed, and she hadn't moved a muscle. When the curtains began to close, and the music stopped, I shot up out of my seat and raced backstage. It took some doing to get back there, but when I finally made it to my baby girl, Aubrielle was kneeling in front of her trying to console her.

"Zee, what's wrong?"

I squatted down to their level, and Zara threw herself into my arms. I couldn't imagine what could have happened that would have her so upset in such a short period of time. When Zara didn't answer me, I asked Aubrielle.

"Did she tell you anything?"

She shook her head. "Just before they went on, we were in the hallway lining up to walk on stage. Zara had to use the bathroom, and I let her go to the one in the hallway. I didn't notice anything when she came out, because we were headed to the stage and she got right back in line."

"Zee, I need you to calm down, baby girl. Tell daddy what's wrong."

It took a few more minutes, but she finally calmed down enough to talk to me.

"Mommy," she said.

"Mommy? What about her? Did you see her?"

She nodded her head, and a fresh round of tears filled her eyes.

"Where, Zee? Where'd you see her?"

"She was in the bathroom. She said she missed me and she wanted to see me dance."

"She's here? She's in this building right now?"

I stood to my full height and headed for the exit.

"Rashaad, where are you going?" Aubrielle shouted.

"To find Carmen."

"No! You can't do that. Now isn't the time. We gotta make sure Zara is okay to perform."

I looked down at my daughter's face, and she was watching me like a hawk. Aubrielle was right. Carmen would have to wait.

"Zee, what else did she say to you?" I got back down to her level so I could look her in her eyes.

"She asked if I missed her, and I told her no because we have Ms. Aubrielle now."

I looked up into Aubrielle's watery eyes, and she immediately looked away from me. I had to fix this shit between us, not just for me, but for Zara, too.

"You said that to her?"

"Yes, Daddy, because you told me to always be honest. Ms. Aubrielle makes you happy, and she makes me happy, too."

"Zee, I don't want you worrying about those things. Okay? No matter what, Daddy will always be here. Can you do me a favor, though?" She nodded. "Can you wipe those tears, go out on that stage, and show everybody that you're a star?"

"Yes, Daddy."

"Okay. I love you."

"I love you, too, Daddy. And you too, Ms. Aubrielle."

27

AUBRIELLE

*J*ust like that, my first ever fall festival had come to an end, and I must say, it was a huge success. Everyone forgot about our short delay, in the beginning, and with good reason. When Zara got back on that stage, she rocked her performance, and it was hard not to focus on only her. She was such an amazing dancer and worked so hard at every rehearsal that I'd given her a cameo in my other two classes' performances. It wasn't my intention, but she messed around and stole the whole show.

All of the dancers were now gathered backstage, listening to Groove Motion owners as they thanked and congratulated them on a successful show. Mr. and Mrs. Cartwright called me to the front of the group. She was holding a bottle of wine while her husband held a bouquet of roses.

"Aubrielle," Mr. Cartwright began. "When we were interviewing for your position, we saw at least twenty candidates. As soon as you walked in, my wife tapped me on the leg and said, 'she's the one.' Of course, by the time the interview was over, I agreed with her one hundred percent. Later on, I asked her how she knew you were the one, and what'd you say, baby?"

"I told him that I felt it in my spirit. Your energy was so welcoming, and everything about your aura told me that you were the one we should hire. Thank God your skills are second to none. We are so blessed to have you."

"Thank you! I feel blessed to be a part of the Groove Motion family."

Everyone cheered and clapped again as they handed me the flowers and wine, followed by hugs. Once that was over, we all headed to the reception that was being held in the multipurpose room, where the families were waiting.

"Ms. Aubrielle, did I do good?" Zara asked as we walked through the crowded hallway.

I guided her to one of the corners where we'd be out of the way and kneeled to her level.

"Zara, you did an outstanding job tonight, and I am so proud of you. The audience loved you so much that you got a standing ovation."

"That's when everybody stands up and cheers and claps?"

"Yes. I know it was hard to focus at first because of what happened but thank you for trying. You deserved all of those cheers and claps, sweetheart."

She wrapped her little arms around my neck and hugged me so tight. It almost brought tears to my eyes. When she released me, she looked at me and said, "You always make me feel good on the inside. My mommy wasn't mean to me, but she didn't make me feel good on the inside."

I had no idea how to respond to that, so I hugged her, and we continued making our way to the reception. I spotted Rashaad and his family, along with Keyla, at a table in the corner.

"Come on. Your dad is over there."

When Zara spotted them, she let go of my hand and ran into her father's arms. By the time I made it to the group, Zara was making her rounds, giving everyone a chance to congratulate her. Everyone in the family was focused on her, except Rashaad. His penetrating gaze was making me feel hot.

"Y'all killed that shi—stuff tonight, cousin!" Keyla said as she put her arm across my shoulders.

"Thank you," I replied to her, with my eyes locked on Rashaad's. "It was fun and exciting, but I'm glad to have two weeks off before the next session starts."

"What are you gonna do with all that free time?" Rashaad asked as he approached me.

He looked so good, wearing a pair of jeans that weren't tight but weren't loose either. The black long-sleeved shirt fit his lean frame perfectly, and the Timbs that completed his outfit made my pussy long for his dick.

"That's my cue. I'm about to head out. I gotta work tonight," Keyla told me before hugging me and whisking away.

"Umm, it's been a long day. I'm gonna say hello to your parents before I do a little mingling."

I tried to walk around him, but he grabbed me around my waist.

"Don't be like that, Elle."

"Rashaad, this isn't the time or the place for us to resolve our issues."

"Are you saying that you want to resolve them?"

"I'm saying if you want to talk, now isn't the time."

"Understood… but we will talk… tonight."

I tried walking around him again to no avail.

"Tonight, Elle. We gon' fix this shit, *tonight*. Now, come meet my son."

I SAT in the living room, waiting for Rashaad to arrive. Before I could get away from his family to mingle with the other parents, he made sure that I met his son, who I immediately fell in love with. I wasn't sure if he planned to get a DNA test or not, but Rashaad Jr. was his twin, and denying him would be pointless. He also made sure that I knew he was coming to see me tonight and had just sent a text, telling me he was on his way.

Not seeing or communicating with him for a full week was pure hell. There were no words to describe how much I missed him. I prayed that Rashaad would be completely honest with me and tell me the whole truth about him and Carmen. I didn't want any more half-truths or surprises. I'd been thinking a lot about our relationship and if I wanted to move forward.

I had to stop focusing on the fact that he lied and tried to figure out *why* he lied. He didn't seem like the lying type, so there had to be a justifiable reason. Rashaad was now the father of two, and one of his children was a newborn. *Would I be able to step in and be a good mother to his children? Did I want to? Who am I fooling?* I already loved Zara like she was my own, and after holding R.J. in my arms for a few seconds, I was head over heels in love with him.

Did I even know how to be a mother? I had so many unanswered questions swirling around in my head, and I had no idea what the answers were to any of them. All I knew was that over the past few months, I envisioned myself becoming his wife, having his babies, and growing old with him, and I still wanted that more than anything else in this world.

The doorbell rang and startled me out of my thoughts. I rushed to answer it, but when I put my hand on the knob, I paused and took a deep breath before pulling it open. There he was, wearing the same outfit from earlier, except now he had on a puffy vest.

When I didn't say anything or invite him in, he said, "You just gon' stare at me all night, or can I come in?"

28

RASHAAD

When she opened the door, I was taken aback by her beauty. Aubrielle was always beautiful, but tonight, she seemed even more so. Maybe it was because I hadn't seen her like this, up close and personal, for several days. Her straight hair was pulled back into a ponytail, and her face was now free of the makeup that she'd worn earlier today. She was wearing one of the many T-shirts that I'd left there with a pair of black leggings. Her feet were bare, exposing her pink toes.

"You just gon' stare at me all night, or can I come in?" I said after a few seconds of admiring her beauty.

Without responding, she moved to the side. I waited for her to lock the door then followed her into the living room. She sat on one end of the couch, and I purposely sat right next to her.

"Rashaad, can you move over some?" she whined, pretending to be annoyed.

"I haven't been this close to you in seven days. You lucky I'm not sitting on top of your ass."

She tucked her legs underneath her and folded her arms across her chest. I adjusted my body so that I was facing her, and she smacked her lips in annoyance. She could go somewhere with that fake mad shit.

"You wanted to talk. I'm listening," she said with an eye roll.

"Are you sure you're ready to listen? I'm not feeling all this attitude you throwing my way."

"Let's talk about *why* I have an attitude."

We had a brief stare down, and I could tell she was fighting to keep her mean face intact.

"I wasn't completely honest with you."

"No shit."

"Chill with all that, Elle. I know I was wrong, but I had my reasons."

I waited to see if she had anything else smart to say, and when she didn't, I continued.

"When my uncle died, I took it hard; harder than the rest of the family. One night I was having a particularly hard time and started drinking. When Carmen came home, I was fucked up. I woke up the next day, and she was in my bed, naked, while I was fully clothed. I woke her up to ask her what the hell was going on. When she told me we had sex, I wanted to wrap my hands around her neck and squeeze until she stopped breathing. That day, I started looking for a house because the setup we had going was gon' have my ass in jail. I blocked that night out of my head and refused to believe it happened. Not long after is when she told me she was leaving."

"She raped you."

"I'm not gon' say all that. A nigga ain't gon' ever admit to being raped by a woman."

"Rashaad, she took advantage of you while you were drunk. If the roles were reversed—"

"Yeah, I know. The shit wasn't cool, but I can't do nothing about it now. All I know is my son was conceived that night, and I'm now the father of two."

"He looks just like you, but umm… did you get a test?"

"The results came back Friday and confirmed what I already knew."

"Wow."

"I apologize for not being completely honest, but if I could do it over, I still wouldn't tell you. It's not something I want to even acknowledge happened. Life has a way of making you deal with things, and Rashaad Jr. is exactly that for me. Regardless of how he got here, he's mine, and I love him just as much as I love Zara."

Tears began to fall from her eyes, and I reached over and cupped her face, using my thumbs to wipe away her tears. I wanted to give her a chance to speak and tell me how she felt, but her response was nothing but silence.

"Elle, talk to me, baby. Tell me that you want to work this out. I don't want to be without you."

After a few sniffles and clearing her throat, she said, "I'm thirty-four years old, and I don't have children."

"I can help you with that."

She blessed me with a weak smile. "I honestly don't know much about taking care of or raising them. When it was just Zara, I was cool because she's older and can tell me what she needs from me."

"But…"

"But now you have a newborn, and the responsibilities that come with being your woman have multiplied. Being with you means going from a single woman with no children to a mother of two, *instantly*."

I didn't like the direction this conversation was headed. I wasn't leaving this house until I convinced her that we could make this shit work.

"There's no parenting manual, Elle. This shit is on-the-job training. When we met, I said that I wasn't looking for someone to be a mother to Zara, but that couldn't be further from the truth. I love you. I need you. Zara loves you and needs you. R.J. doesn't know it yet, but he loves you and needs you, too."

"Rashaad, this is too much. I don't know if I can—"

I got on my knees in front of her because I wasn't above begging. This woman had become a part of me in a short period of time, and I didn't want to lose her.

"Please, baby. Don't do this to me. I love you with everything in me, and I *know* my forever is with you. There's no one else in this world that I want by my side as I go through this life."

"I love you, too."

I reached inside the puffy vest that I was wearing and pulled out a little blue box.

"Do you love me enough to become Mrs. Rashaad Khalil Hanes?"

EPILOGUE

One Year Later

29

AUBRIELLE

"What are you doing here?" Rashaad asked when he opened the door to his office.

"I wanted to see you. Is that okay?"

"It's more than okay."

He kissed my forehead before stepping to the side and pulling the door open a little wider, giving me room to enter. I headed straight for the couch that we'd created some great memories on in the past.

"You busy?" I asked once I was seated comfortably. He sat next to me, leaving very little room between us, then turned his body toward mine.

"Never too busy for you. Wassup?"

"Nothing, really." I honestly had no reason to be there besides wanting to see him.

"You missing a nigga, huh. You been having withdrawal symptoms. At home fiending for some of this milk chocolate."

"Boy, ain't nobody fiending for you." I rolled my eyes, even though he was right. Just being this close to him had my panties wet.

"Are you sure about that, Elle? You know I know you better than I know myself. Your pheromones been tossing me signals since I opened the door. Is there something you need from me?"

"Rashaad—"

Before I could lie to him, he grabbed the back of my neck and smashed his lips against mine. I didn't have the strength nor the desire to resist him, so I sank into the kiss. When his tongue brushed my lips, requesting entrance into my mouth, I greedily allowed access.

The passion behind his kiss let me know he was hungry for me, that he craved me as much as I craved him. He slipped his hand underneath my shirt and spent some time caressing my stomach before he moved up to my breasts. The way we were positioned wasn't conducive to what we both wanted to happen, so without disconnecting his mouth from mine, he pulled me to my feet.

Without warning, our connection was broken, and he turned me around, yanking my sweats down from the back and taking my underwear with them. I could hear him unbuckling his belt, unzipping his pants, and the rustling sound of them falling to the floor.

"Hold on to the arm of the couch," he demanded.

He entered me with a gentle force, causing me to bite my bottom lip but still unable to stifle my moaning.

"Damn, Elle. She was wet and ready for me."

His dick slid in and out, in repeated brisk movements. For some reason, he was being gentle, but I wanted it hard.

"Fuck me, baby. Fuck me hard," I told him.

"Say no more."

His hands gripped the sides of my waist, and I felt him dip at the knees. The pounding began and almost immediately sent my libido to another level. Reaching around my body, his digits found my clit, and he applied just the right amount of pressure. I loved how well he knew my body. It never to him long to bring me to my peak. Today was no different.

"Shit! Rashaad, I'm cummin'!" I screamed.

As my pussy pulsed around his dick, I felt a huge gush of fluid.

"Damn, Elle! You feel like a damn waterfall today."

"Oh my God! Baby, I think my water just broke."

You would think that would've alarmed him, but this nigga was close to his nut and did not let up until he emptied all of his seeds inside of me.

"This pussy is phenomenal, baby. Now, what was that you said?"

"I said my water broke!"

"Oh shit!"

He abruptly pulled out of me and helped me position myself on the couch. My sweats were still around my knees, so my lower half was exposed.

"Does it hurt? Are you in pain? Where's my phone? I gotta call the ambulance."

Rashaad was in a bit of a panic as he spat out questions with his pants still at his ankles and his dick flopping around.

"Baby, calm down. Pull your pants up and help me get mine up."

He nodded nervously but did as he was told. Once our lower extremities were covered, I said, "Help me up and get me to the hospital."

"Are you sure? Can you walk? Do I need to carry—"

"Baby!" I shouted. "Look at me. Calm down. The baby—owww, shit! That hurt."

"The fuck, Elle. I knew I shouldn't have listened to your ass! Talking about fuck you hard. You see what the fuck happened?"

"Ahhh, baby, this hurts bad. Call the—oh my God!"

I held my stomach while Rashaad found his phone. My eyes were closed, and I took deep breaths through the contractions that came out of nowhere and were coming fast and hard. I listened as he called 911 and requested an ambulance, telling them his wife was in labor. The phone was on speaker, and when the voices got closer, I opened my eyes and saw that Rashaad had placed the phone on the table and was kneeling on the floor next to me.

"Sir, I've dispatched an ambulance to your location, and it should be there soon. How far apart are her contractions?"

"I don't know. They started all of a sudden and got bad real quick."

While all of this is going on, I was moaning and groaning in pain. I began to cry because it was almost unbearable.

"Oh my God! There's too much pressure! I think the baby is coming!"

"What! Noooo, baby, you gotta wait for the ambulance."

"Sir, can you see if the baby is crowning?" the operator asked.

"What the hell is that?"

"Is the baby coming out?"

"She said it feels like it. Hang on!"

He got up and ran to his office door. After fumbling with the door, he screamed at the top of his lungs, "Somebody help! Elle's having the baby!"

"Ma'am, can you hear me?" the operator began to direct her questions to me.

"Yes," I breathed as Rashaad maneuvered my sweats back down my legs.

"Oh my fucking God! I see the baby's head. Where the hell is the ambulance?" he shouted.

"Sir, please try to calm down. It will help keep your wife calm."

"Ma'am, my son's head is sticking out of my wife's pussy. I'm not a damn doctor. How the hell am I supposed to be calm?"

"Rashaad, what's going—oh, damn. Aubrielle, you in labor?" Rasheeda said when she walked in.

"Sheeda, the baby's head is right there," he informed her.

"Oh, God. Did you call the ambulance?" Rasheeda paced back and forth nervously.

"I can't—I have to push—babyyyyy—help me. It hurt—it hurts so bad."

"Sheeda, come hold her hand. I gotta—"

"Ahhhhh!" I screamed. "I think he's—baby, do you see—I feel—oh, God, please!"

"Hold her hand, Sheeda. I gotta pull the baby out."

"What?"

"Come here! You gotta help."

Rashaad put one of my legs on the back of the couch and told Rasheeda to hold the other up.

"Come on, Elle. His head is halfway out. You gotta keep pushing," Rashaad said.

"It hurts too much," I cried.

"You gotta push, baby. It might feel better when he comes out."

As I gathered enough energy to give one more good push, the past year of my life flashed through my mind.

"Do you love me enough to become Mrs. Rashaad Khalil Hanes?"

"What?"

"Will you be my wife and the mother of my children? Not just Zara and R.J., but the ones I plant inside of you, too, baby."

"You want to get married and have more kids?"

"Yes, a whole tribe of them as long as it's with you. Now will you marry a nigga or what, Elle?"

"Yes, Rashaad. I'll marry you."

Within a few weeks, I moved in with him, and I couldn't lie, adjusting to my new life almost took me out. Mrs. Hanes was a Godsend and had the patience of Job. If it weren't for her constant presence and the nonstop Face-Time calls to my mother, I would have given up. It took me a couple of months to adapt to taking care of a family, and it was a blessing to have my mother and soon-to-be mother-in-law guiding me along the way.

Six months after he proposed, our wedding and reception were held at the skating rink, and it would go down in history as the dopest event to ever take place in Washington D.C. Yep, I said it. Rasheeda was our wedding planner, and she outdid herself. The theme was Roll Bounce Love, and our colors were gold and white. The soundtrack of the night was nothing but hits for the eighties and nineties. If that wasn't enough, Rasheeda was able to get Donnie Simpson to be the MC of our reception. So when I said it would go down in history, I meant it.

Everyone in the wedding party, which only consisted of Rashawn as the best man, Keyla as the maid of honor, and Zara as the flower girl, wore roller skates, including us. Rashawn and Keyla were so hot and cold with each other that pairing them up was almost a disaster, but I was grateful they called a truce for our special day.

My daddy and I were still at odds and weren't able to resolve our issues before the wedding. Even though Rashaad and I explained to him how R.J.

was conceived, he didn't trust Rashaad and was adamant about him not being good enough for me. He thought the only reason Rashaad wanted to get married was to have someone to take care of his kids.

Needless to say, when I saw my daddy standing at the end of the makeshift aisle, I broke down. We hadn't spoken in months, and it didn't seem as if our relationship would ever be repaired. I loved my daddy, but he was wrong about Rashaad, and I refused to lose out on the man I loved because he wanted to be stubborn. My heart was soaring by the time I made it to my dad, and I cried like a baby in his embrace. Shout out to my makeup artist for getting me back together real quick.

When we returned from our honeymoon in Bermuda, I was sick as a dog. We thought I had caught a bug while traveling, only to find out that I was a little over three months pregnant. I had absolutely no clue, because I had no symptoms, and my cycle didn't stop until I was five months along.

Here I was, six months after becoming Mrs. Rashaad Khalil Hanes, giving birth to his second son, in the place that we first met. Crazy how things came full circle.

30

RASHAAD

I sat in the rocking chair in the corner of the hospital room, cradling my son in my arms. Khalil Abraham Hanes came into this world kicking and screaming, at a whopping ten pounds and twenty-two inches long. I could already tell that his personality wasn't gonna be as laid back as his brother's. My uncle Abraham would be honored to have him as his namesake.

I still couldn't believe that I delivered my son on that same couch that he was probably conceived. When I told Aubrielle to give me one last push, she must have dug deep for that strength. Khalil's head popped out, and I was able to pull his big ass out the rest of the way.

The paramedics barged into my office just in time because I had no idea what to do after that. I was still not sure how they knew where to find us, but I was glad they did. Rasheeda and I moved out of the way, and they took over. It only took us a few minutes to get to the hospital, so I wasn't sure why the hell it took them so long to get to the skating rink. All was well now, so I wouldn't dwell on all that.

Khalil began to squirm and turned his face toward my chest, smacking his lips. I knew exactly what that meant, and I hated to wake Aubrielle up, but I couldn't do shit for my lil' homie.

"Baby," I whispered. "Baby, wake up."

She opened her eyes and smiled weakly.

"He's looking for you."

She adjusted her gown and reached for him. After placing him in her arms, Khalil barely waited for her to position him before he was attacking her breast.

"Damn, son. You know those belong to me."

"Not anymore," Aubrielle said. "You gon' have to find something else to suck on for a while."

I shook my head in defeat. "I guess it's a small sacrifice for my legacy. He better appreciate that shit, too."

I kissed her forehead and went back to the rocking chair. My phone vibrated on the windowsill, and I picked it up, looking at the screen. It was flooded with text messages and missed calls. The only people I replied to were our parents, my siblings, Keyla, and of course, Zara. She was anxious to see her new baby brother and would probably be calling me soon to find out when that would be happening.

I watched my wife as she fed our newborn son. The way she looked down at him while he got his nourishment from her body made me fall in love with her a little bit more if that was possible. I'd been wanting to ask her something for a few months, but for some reason, it never felt like the right time. But right there, right then, was perfect.

"Baby?"

"Hmm?" she replied without looking away from Khalil.

"I love you."

Then she looked at me and smiled. "I love you, too, baby." Her eyes went back to our son.

Walking over to the bed, I pulled an envelope out of my back pocket.

"Zara and R.J. love you, too. The way you stepped in and assumed the role of their mother and how you embraced the idea of Zara calling you mommy is something I can never thank you enough for. I know you were afraid you wouldn't be good enough, but you—you've been—you are *everything* to us."

"Baby, don't make me cry. This day has been emotional enough as it is."

"I know, but there's something I've been wanting to ask you for a few months. I wanted to find the perfect time, and this is it."

"What is it, Rashaad? You're making me nervous."

"I want to make it official."

She looked confused and asked, "Make what official? We're already married."

"In this envelope is the paperwork we need to start the process of adoption. I want you to adopt Zara and R.J."

She gasped and put her free hand over her mouth as tears poured from her eyes.

"It would mean everything to me and even more to them. In our hearts and minds, you are their mother. You chose to be here, and you chose to love them. I don't want there to be any questions or doubts in your mind about your place in their lives."

"Baby, I didn't have to choose to love them, because it came naturally. I love them as if you planted them in my belly and I nurtured them in my womb for nine months. My love for them is no different than my love for Khalil. For you to give me this gift means that you know that my love for them is true and pure. That means everything to me. I would love to adopt Zara and Rashaad Jr."

She was still holding Khalil, but he had fallen asleep. I took him from her arms, placed him in the bassinet next to her bed, and then walked around to the other side. Slipping off my shoes, I crawled in behind her, gently wrapping my arms around her.

"Since the moment I laid eyes on you, you have been a ray of light in my life. I didn't think there was anything that could make me happier than you taking my last name. But this… this made me love you more than I ever thought possible. I love you so much, Elle."

"I love you, too, Rashaad."

Our relationship was on a *roll*, and although we hit a few bumps along the way, we were able to *bounce* back, and now, it was nothing but *love*.

THE END

AFTERWORD

Dear Readers,

 I hope you enjoyed Rashaad and Aubrielle's story. I wanted to give you something fun and sexy, with a little drama. I hope I delivered. Thank you all for continuing to encourage and support my work. If you could please leave a review on Amazon and/or Goodreads, I would greatly appreciate it. Until next time. Also, search Roll Bounce Love on Spotify to enjoy the playlist.

Kay Shanee

LET'S CONNECT!

You can find me at all of the following:
Reading Group: Kay Shanee's Reading Korner – After Dark Facebook page: Author Kay Shanee
Instagram: @AuthorKayShanee
Goodreads: Kay Shanee
Subscribe to my mailing list: Subscribe to Kay Shanee Website Order Signed Paperbacks: www.AuthorKayShanee.com

OTHER BOOKS BY KAY SHANEE

STANDALONES

Love Hate and Everything in Between

Love Doesn't Hurt

Love Unconventional

I'd Rather Be With You

Can't Resist This Complicated Love

Love's Sweet Serenade

COMPLETED SERIES

Until the Wheels Fall Off

Until the Wheels Fall Off...Again

Could This Be Love ~ Part 1
Could This Be Love ~Part 2

SPIN-OFF SERIES

The Love I Deserve
Loving Him Through the Storm
Since the Day We Met
Easy to Love
Heal My Heart
To Have Her Again

Visit bit.ly/readBLP to join our mailing list!
Let's connect on social media!
Facebook - B. Love Publications
Twitter - @blovepub
Instagram - @blovepublications

Made in the USA
Las Vegas, NV
23 September 2021